WITHDRAWN

# FITZCARRALDO

## The
## Original
## Story

*by*

# Werner Herzog

*Translated
from the German by*
Martje Herzog
*and*
Alan Greenberg

F J O R D   P R E S S
S A N   F R A N C I S C O
1 9 8 2

Title of original German edition: *Fitzcarraldo*
Copyright © 1982 Carl Hanser Verlag München Wien

Photo credits
Front cover:  Werner Herzog Filmproduktion and Schirmer/Mosel Verlag,
München
Map:  Werner Herzog Filmproduktion, München
Back cover:  copyright © 1982 Maureen Gosling

Our thanks to Lucki Stipetić, Maureen Gosling, and Les Blank

Editors:  Steven T. Murray & Susan Doran
Cover design:  John Heisch

Published and distributed by:
Fjord Press
P.O. Box 615
Corte Madera, California  94925

Library of Congress Cataloging in Publication Data:
Catalog Card No.: 82-82673
Herzog, Werner, 1942—
   Fitzcarraldo. The original story.
San Francisco, CA: Fjord Press
160 p.
ISBN: 0-940242-04-4

Printed in the United States of America
First edition, October 1982
9   8   7   6   5   4   3   2   1

# Fitzcarraldo

*The
Original
Story*

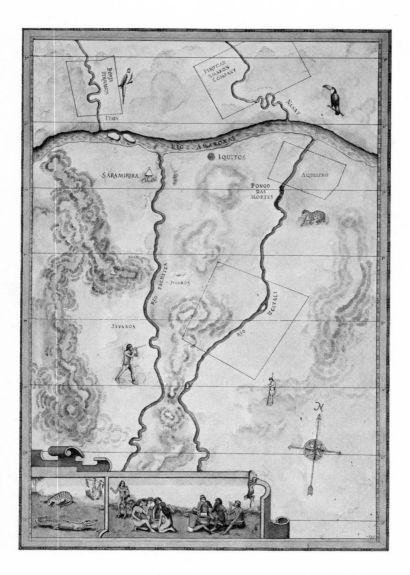

## Foreword

The fundamental geographical pattern is vitally important for the understanding of this text. The two tributaries of the Amazon, the Pachitea and the Ucayali, do exist, but in reality their course is completely different from the description in this story. Their names have been selected only for their sound.

Only one thing matters for the story: both of them are tributaries of the Amazon, running roughly parallel to one another. In one place, far along their upper course, the rivers come very close to each other. The Pachitea flows into the Amazon upstream from the city of Iquitos, the Ucayali downstream. The upper course of the Ucayali would be easily navigable if the Pongo das Mortes rapids did not block the flow early on.

The Pongo das Mortes really exists, although in actuality it is called Pongo de Manseriche and is situated on the upper course of the Río Marañón.

# Characters

| | |
|---|---|
| *Enrico Caruso* | |
| *Brian Sweeney Fitzgerald* | called Fitzcarraldo |
| *Wilbur* | his nephew, feebleminded |
| *Bronski* | actor |
| *Molly* | former singer |
| *Jaime de Aguila* | captain |
| *Huerequeque* | cook |
| *Stan* | juggler |
| *The Mechanic* | |
| *Don Aquilino* | rubber baron |
| *Don Araujo* | rubber baron |
| *The Borja Brothers* | rubber barons |
| *Notary* | |
| *Opera Director* | |
| *Black Lackey* | |
| *McNamara* | 11-year-old Jívaro boy |
| *Jesuit Missionaries* | |

*Inhabitants of Iquitos, Manaus and Belén; Jívaro Indians*

plus *Gringo* and *Verdi*, Fitzcarraldo's dogs, and *Bald Eagle*, his parrot

## Manaus, Teatro Amazonas, Night

The big, pompous opera house is festively illuminated, a row of elegant carriages stretches all the way up the ramp, which is beautifully ornamented with light and dark inlaid bricks. The clay-caked spokes of the wheels, in which huge jungle leaves have been caught here and there, and the horses' hooves give us the first hint that the opera has been built in the middle of nowhere, in a jungle settlement suddenly become rich.

In front of the gigantic portal, two Indian palace guards stand wearing uniforms from the wars of liberation. Their glances are wrapped in jungle trance, far from all comprehension. By the carriages, black servants in gala livery, hands gloved white, are standing in wait. A distinguished-looking gentleman with a top hat and black cape, who apparently has arrived a bit late, hastens toward the portal. "Champagne for the horses," he hurriedly calls to his servant. The latter hangs a bucket on the drawbar and actually fills it with several bottles of the choicest French champagne. The horse slurps it up.

From the jungle, which can't be far, cicadas shout their monotonous song of the night; from inside the foyer of the opera house we hear the typical mixture of festive murmuring and the orchestra tuning its instruments. Apart from this, we hear only the pawing and chewing of the horses. Only the champagne-drenched horse disturbs the pattern, accompanying his lapping with a patient, long-drawn-out, long-range fart. Otherwise all is quiet. The horse makes a deadpan face. With the sound of a kettle drum, the overture to Verdi's *A Masked Ball* begins inside.

Closer to the portal. Full of awe, some curious on-lookers — various barefooted half-breeds, along with *caucheros,* the local rubber workers, in tattered pants, and a few mulattos from the poorer quarters — have formed an impassable wall.

They are staring inside, listening intently to the music, which meanwhile has opened up fully and oozes outward in muffled tones. Only the liveried servants near the horses think themselves better and loll on the upholstery of the carriages. Near the wall of closely-packed people, under a glass showcase, a huge poster proclaims in big letters: *Enrico Caruso* and *Sarah Bernhardt* together in a sensational *Gala Performance* on the stage of the *Teatro Amazonas, Manaus*; and below, in much smaller print: *A Masked Ball,* by Giuseppe Verdi.

## Manaus, Harbor, Night

The moonlight reflects off a lake so wide we cannot make out the far shore, and the lake moves. It is the monstrous middle stretch of the Amazon River. At the edge, dozens of boats of all sizes, most of them for cargo, are moored. Many of the boats have roofs of corrugated tin or braided palm fronds, and next to them lie cargo rafts made of balsa wood for cattle transport. A tree trunk comes float-ing by, and directly after it a *peke-peke* emerges, one of those typical Amazon boats that appeared shortly after the turn of the century, with a simple gasoline engine, covered by a palm roof.

The engine does not work, and we see Fitzcarraldo, strenuously rowing the boat with one paddle against the current, then tying up on land. Wilbur is steering at the stern. Both wear white linen suits, but Fitzcarraldo's is visibly soiled with sweat and dark, oily spots. His hands are wrapped in dirty bandages soaked with blood and oil. He wears a battered straw hat, although the sun went down a long time ago.

Wilbur is trying to heave a magnificent barber chair off the boat, a chair that could only have been invented around the turn of the century in a Latin country. But Fitzcarraldo urges him on insistently. "My God," he says, "we're too late."


## Teatro Amazonas, Stage

The opera has reached its climax. The production, seen from the audience, is bombastic in the extreme, overstylized. The turn of the century celebrates itself.

It is the gloomy night scene, where Amelia timidly approaches the high court to look for the magic herb under the gallows. Theater lightning flashes through the fearsome landscape. Sarah Bernhardt, as Amelia, is clearly limping; her flowing costume cannot conceal that she has a wooden leg. Neither does she sing herself, but only moves her lips. Down in the orchestra pit stands a real singer, singing the aria "If the herb, as the fortune teller says . . ." for her.

Enrico Caruso, as Riccardo, who has followed her, urges her to confess her love. Their feelings for each other flare up in a blaze of wild passion in the duet "I am close to you," while, unnoticed by the two of them, the plotters lurk in the gloom of their hiding-place. Suddenly Renato, Amelia's husband, appears to warn Lord Riccardo of the conspirators. Amelia just manages to pull the folds of her veil over her face. The men exchange cloaks, and Riccardo leaves, as Renato begs him to, but demands from the latter an oath that he will escort the veiled lady to the gates of the city without speaking a word.

Then his path is barred by the plotters, the black-guards, who demand to see the lady's face. . . .

### Manaus, Quay, Night

Fitzcarraldo and Wilbur hasten along the quay, where amid the clay and muck a few miserable bars thrown together with old boards serve sugarcane rotgut, where stuporous drunks play cards, where prostitutes of the cheapest kind loiter about. One of them blocks Fitzcarraldo's way. "Hola!" she says. "Gringo!" But he shuns her and hurries on. In his haste he has brought his paddle with him.

## Teatro Amazonas, Night

As before, the ragged, barefoot figures form a wall, as they listen intently to the sounds inside. The opera seems to be drawing slowly to a close; a dramatic climax of delusion, death, and belated recognition builds. When Fitzcarraldo and Wilbur come running up, panting, the faces turn. Fitzcarraldo stops short when he realizes everyone is staring at his paddle. He is embarrassed for a moment because it is so out of place. Pulling himself together, he puts on a small face and pulls Wilbur through the wall of gaping people into the foyer.

## Teatro Amazonas, Foyer

A festive radiance illuminates the huge, columned foyer. The marble floor reflects the lights from the crystal chandeliers. On the walls all around are garish jungle paintings with the lurking jaguar and other Amazonian imagery. At once, an elderly black man in particularly splendid livery bars the way of the two intruders.

"Gentlemen," he says in a refined tone of voice, "you may not enter here — this is a gala." With a condescending look he assesses the strangers' clothes and paddle.

"The Barber of Seville?" asks Wilbur. "Figaro?"

Fitzcarraldo composes himself; he's going to put everything on the line. "We have been traveling ten days. We've come down the Amazon fifteen hundred kilometers from Iquitos. Two days ago our engine broke down. Look at this. Look at our hands! We've been rowing two days and two nights, just to see Caruso for once in our lives — the great Caruso, *the one and only — in person.*"

"Excuse me," says the black man in a friendlier tone of voice, "you have no tickets, and this performance has been sold out for six months."

"Please," implores Fitzcarraldo, "we have to get in. I once had my own theater, and *I have to get in here.* I too am going to erect an opera house, in Iquitos, and Caruso is going to inaugurate it. The plans are all set. It will be the greatest opera the jungle has ever seen, and I am going to name you as Administrative Director if you let me in now." More and more urgently he insists, for, inside, the agony of the grand finale is already in the air.

"I myself would like to be inside," says the black man, and Fitzcarraldo senses that the ice has broken at last. "Make sure to be very quiet," says the black man, "and squeeze against the wall back there by the entrance."

"Figaro!" says Wilbur, "The Barber of Seville!" A joy known only to the feeble-minded radiates from within, illuminating him.


*Teatro Amazonas, Auditorium*

Red velvet and gilded chandeliers. Three tiers of balcony tower one above the other. This opera house was begotten in lust. Breathless silence reigns. On the apron of the stage, hardly visible because he is lying on the floor in the throes of death, is Caruso as Lord Riccardo, wearing the disguise of a harlequin for the masked ball. Sarah Bernhardt, who as Amelia has now discarded her shrouds, has thrown herself upon him, rather clumsily due to her wooden leg, but nevertheless in utter exaltation.

The conductor is an imperious Italian with the look of a military commander in his eyes. Beneath him stands the singer, who sings Bernhardt's part, while up on the stage Bernhardt merely mouths the words.

Caruso, the dying man, in the robes of the harlequin, raises himself for the last time for an aria. Leaning on his elbow, he hands his murderer Renato a document guaranteeing him his friendship and the inviolability of his honor. With his last words he forgives his murderers and hails his homeland. Caruso flings out his right hand, indicating an imaginary distance, where the horizon lies, the other bank of the river, vaguely in the direction where Fitzcarraldo stands.

Fitzcarraldo has pressed himself against the rear wall. He clutches his paddle with his sore fist. He has removed his hat as well. There he stands, the man, the *witness of the sublime*. Caruso's grand gesture from the stage pierces him like a lance.

"He was pointing at you," Wilbur whispers to him.

Then the mighty curtain falls, with its colossal allegorical painting of the birth of the Amazon River. Only the turn of the century and the rutting imagination of the jungle could have given birth to such a monstrous allegory. Tremendous applause surges upward in foaming waves. Lights, festive glamour, cheers, bows, curtain calls. Fitzcarraldo alone stands frozen like a pillar of salt.

Then, finally, the applause ebbs away, and the first spectators leave the auditorium. Long evening gowns, jewels, tuxedos, and starched shirtfronts. They press toward the exit where Fitzcarraldo stands weeping in his rumpled linen suit with his bloody hands, paddle in his fist. Disapproving glances; people feel disturbed by Fitzcarraldo's display of emotion. Wilbur doesn't quite know what to do, and casts a troubled glance at Fitzcarraldo. Then, caught by the same emotion, Wilbur too begins to weep. The loneliness of what they have just experienced unites the two, forges their bond, the secret of which we can only guess.

## Teatro Amazonas, Office of the Director

The ostentatious office of the director, a stout man with an alert intelligence and a sentimental bent. He is seated behind his mahogany desk, on which is one of the very first telephones, along with framed photographs of opera singers with autographs, a potted palm next to them, orchids in a sumptuous vase. Fitzcarraldo and Wilbur are sitting across from him; they have been offered tiny cups of black mocha.

"Fitzcarraldo?" asks the director with feigned astonishment.

"Let me explain," says Fitzcarraldo. "My father was an Irishman, and my real name is Fitzgerald. Brian Sweeney Fitzgerald. But in Peru nobody could pronounce my name correctly, so I modified it a bit."

"Fitzgerald? Iquitos?" wonders the opera director. "You're not by any chance the man with the railroad?"

"Yes," admits Fitzcarraldo, somewhat embarrassed, "the Trans-Andean Railway from the Amazon over the Andes to the coast of the Pacific. But that enterprise, as you certainly have heard, fell through. At the moment I am trying my luck as an ice manufacturer in order to raise some money. I'm only doing it because I have but one dream, the opera: *the Grand Opera in the jungle.* I am going to build it, and Caruso will inaugurate it!"

"Yes, Caruso," echoes Wilbur devotedly.


*Teatro Amazonas, Backstage*

The opera director conducts his visitors backstage, where the sets have been taken away minutes earlier. "Our house might be too small in a couple of years," he tells them. "For five years now we've been the richest city in the world."

"And Iquitos," adds Fitzcarraldo, "is catching up. As far as rubber is concerned, we have almost reached the same production figures."

"This place is getting a little crazy," says the director. "Our prices are now four times as high as in New York;

19

palaces are being built with tiles from Delft and marble from Florence. We have a telephone network with three hundred connections, more than Paris. And the people who are more well-to-do, if I may use that expression, send their laundry to be done in Lisbon, because the water in the Amazon is felt to be too impure. Unfortunately, our governor Ribeiro has died . . ."

"What?" says Fitzcarraldo, "he couldn't have been more than thirty years old."

"You know, between ourselves, although the newspapers gave a different version of the incident," the director replies mysteriously, "he strangled himself in a fit of erotic frenzy." Then he adds in a more formal tone, "Our governor Ribeiro said at the inauguration of this house: 'If the growth of this city calls for it, we will tear down this opera house and build a bigger one.' This one was put right in the middle of the jungle — now see how the city has grown up around it."


## Teatro Amazonas, On Stage

Fitzcarraldo, Wilbur, the director, and the uniformed man from the night before wander through the auditorium; without people it now seems much vaster but no longer as festive and glamourous. Nevertheless, this theater is unique in the entire world. Wilbur feels the velvet upholstery of the seats and tries out several, one after another.

Fitzcarraldo, who addresses the black man as "Mr. Administrative Director," tests the hall's acoustics from the stage, shouting Ho! and Ha! and clapping his hands, listening to the echo.

## Dressing Room

Inside the dressing room used by Caruso just shortly before, Fitzcarraldo is noticeably quiet, impressed.

"Do you know how much Caruso got for this one evening?" the director asks. "Two hundred thousand gold escudos," he answers himself. "And Sarah Bernhardt almost twice as much, though she can't even sing, but the public here wanted both of them at once."

"Where has my nephew gone?" asks Fitzcarraldo. "Have you seen Wilbur?"

## Teatro Amazonas, On Stage

Fitzcarraldo and the black man find Wilbur cowering in a chair in the middle of the stage, frightened, like a nocturnal animal suddenly blinded by a searchlight. Fitzcarraldo tries to see what Wilbur sees. But there is only the yawning void of the empty auditorium, with its row upon row of empty seats, staring back motionless, expectant, as if the people to fill them were unnecessary. Then there are the big fans, with their long, long, rotating wooden blades twitching as they turn. "This man here knows what a stage is," says Fitzcarraldo.

## Amazon River, Toward Evening

Gigantic, almost motionless, the vast river is resting in itself. Calmly and surely, Fitzcarraldo's boat follows its course. Upstream, to the west, the heavens are lit by the glowing red light of the evening sky. Steam sinks down upon the jungle. Parrots fly in flocks over the boat, squawking in their typically restless flight. Quiet and composed, Wilbur and Fitzcarraldo sit and steer the boat against the current, into the night. Wilbur is stretched out comfortably in his barber chair, his feet propped up on the footrest.

## Tres Cruces, Dawn

Their backs to us, as in an old painting, Fitzcarraldo and Wilbur sit and survey a visionary land now resting in the mythical mists of early morning. They are on the last heights of the Andes, from which the jungle descends into the immeasurable expanse of the Amazon basin. Into unimaginable depths the jungle ripples out to where sight gives out and vision begins. The view is beyond compare; in the whole of South America there is nothing like it. As immense as an ocean extending to the edges of the universe, the jungle stretches out, steaming, as on the morning of Creation, still indistinct, full of animal noise. A music swells up, magnificent, breathtaking, and measured, as a hundred million birds awaken far below our feet. The earth lies in wait, calmly and patiently, but the sky begins to quiver as if this were some painful quaking of the heavens, something like the birth throes of heaven.

Softly, almost hesitantly, Fitzcarraldo begins to speak. He seems to be seeking a measure for the immeasurable. "From here," he says, "it's four thousand kilometers to the Atlantic. Do you know what the Indians call the jungle? They call it *the dreamland,* and here, where the rapids are, they call it *the land God created in wrath.* We shall bring Grand Opera to this place, this is where it must happen."

"How?" asks Wilbur. "How are you going to do it?"

"I don't know yet," says Fitzcarraldo. "Listen now, hold your breath and don't move."

The horizon erupts into convulsions and, bathed in trembling flames, it now gives birth to a sun, a wavering, gigantic ball of red, breathing fire, bigger than we have ever seen the sun before.

## Iquitos, Riverbank and City Streets

Even this first glimpse of the city makes us aware of the enormous gap between Fitzcarraldo's dream and its realization. His boat is moored in an awful jumble of other boats; there are rafts loaded with cattle for the slaughterhouse and others piled high with fruit. A cow has broken loose and swims out into the current, pursued by a man with a liana rope.

The hillside up to the town is strewn with fermenting garbage; vultures, pigs, and naked children poke about in it as equals. The vultures, hundreds of them, are black, sluggish, and ugly, waiting for the entrails and steaming refuse from the slaughterhouse, where every day the murdering seems to begin anew.

Farther up are the first wind-warped shacks, roofed with corrugated tin, where dingy bars dispense sugarcane booze to men who, in the early hours of morning, lie drunk in their own urine. Rice and yucca and bananas are frying and simmering everywhere, on the boats and up on the street on improvised fireplaces. Timber of tremendous girth is hauled ashore; women squat fully dressed in the river, doing their wash; rubbish gathers in whirlpools around the bows of the boats; some children torment a mangy dog in a doorway. *Peke-pekes* ride the river, up and down, Indians stagger under the overly heavy loads balanced on their backs with the aid of head straps, people jostle each other, Indian women suckle their children, people sleep on precarious planks. This is a place where chaos will triumph over order for all eternity.

We see Fitzcarraldo and Wilbur as they work their way up to the town, through the slippery clay on the slope that keeps crumbling away. An Indian porter has loaded Wilbur's barber chair onto his back.

We accompany Fitzcarraldo through one or two streets. We can see clearly that Iquitos has been wrested from the jungle only in the last few years. Low houses with sheet-metal roofs, loitering beggars, loitering *caucheros,* loitering dogs — the dogs are truly the most wretched to be found on this earth. Everywhere there are signs of rubber, the gold that has made everything possible here. Lined up in heavy bales along the edge of the streets, the rubber awaits transport, watched over by fifteen-year-old Indian guards armed with carbines — children who understand nothing, only that they must instantly open fire on anything nearing the goods. Vultures crouch on the rooftops, glutted by carrion and the sweltering heat. In the streets there is the hustle and bustle of life, but it is overshadowed by fatigue, fever, disillusionment, and poverty. In the background, where all the streets end at the Amazon, the palaces of the rich are situated, bombastic, their outer walls set with colored tiles.

## Belén District, Fitzcarraldo's Hut, Morning

Fitzcarraldo wakes up in his hammock, blinking his eyes without opening them, pretending to go on sleeping. He knows his audience has already arrived, has been waiting patiently for a long time. Like a silent, enclosing wall the Indian children stand at a respectful distance. Among them an unusually long-legged, woolly pig, a real sprinter, has pushed its way to the front in breathless curiosity.

Drunk with sleep, Fitzcarraldo gropes with one hand toward a little table, as if it were wandering away in a dream, upon which sits one of the very earliest phonographs. It is one of Edison's machines with needle and horn which, in those days, worked by sensing the grooved cylinder. The machine starts to move, the morning concert begins: these are the first recordings of Enrico Caruso, terribly scratchy, but of an unspeakably dignified beauty, sad and strong and moving.

Fitzcarraldo now opens his eyes completely. "When one day my opera house is built, you will have your own box and an armchair covered in velvet," he tells the pig. It stands there as if rooted to the ground, listening.

Now we see Fitzcarraldo's hut more closely. It rests on tall poles, like hundreds of others around it. Through the slits in the floor we see people moving underneath. The hut is extremely simple, essentially a platform, almost without walls and covered with a braided roof. From his house we can see through dozens of similar huts: one always participates in the lives of one's neighbors. Some of the houses rest on thick, rotting balsa logs so that when the water rises, they float. Nearby runs a narrow tributary of the Amazon, upon which there is busy boat traffic.

## *Belén, Fitzcarraldo's Porch, Later That Morning*

Fitzcarraldo has gathered his followers and is sipping black coffee with them. First we must introduce his two dogs, Gringo and Verdi, the ultimate monstrosities of misery. He treats them, however, like aristocratic greyhounds, talking to them now and then in a tongue especially invented by himself. But his most splendid companion is Bald Eagle, a relatively small, previously green parrot that now has only a few feathers left on its body; both the back of its head and its ass are completely bald. He apparently has been trying for some time to teach the bird two sentences in particular, with only moderate success: "I am an eagle, yes I am," and "Birds are smart but they cannot speak."

Stan has arrived, a young, pleasant-looking juggler, bearded and slender, always looking a little shy. He has an unmistakable New York accent. Wilbur has placed his coffee cup on the floor and is busy feeding his snake, which he keeps in a glass cage. The snake is one of those rare specimens born with two heads. Both heads are fighting each other for the food.

"It's possible," Fitzcarraldo muses, "that we could sell the use of the patent. Just imagine the possibilities. Ice!

Ice on every boat, in every storehouse, and to cool your mattresses at night."

"But," Stan interjects, "why doesn't anyone take this seriously?"

"The potato wasn't taken seriously for two hundred years," says Fitzcarraldo. "It's going to drive me crazy! We've got to prove that people need ice, then we'll find a backer. Just think, we could supply Colombia, Ecuador."

"In the States," Stan says, "they've already flown fifty miles with powered airplanes, and people still don't want any ice."


## Belén, Fitzcarraldo's Ice Factory

At the outskirts of Belén, where the steps go up to the town of Iquitos and where the teeming Indian market starts, there are log houses with corrugated tin roofs that are built somewhat more solidly, yet are unable to disguise their slovenly, temporary, Amazonian character. The side facing the market is half open, and life outside surges past. Stands with roofs of canvas or tin, men and children laden with cargo, fish kept fresh by sprinkling water on it, meat beneath clusters of whirring flies, fruit, heaps of garbage, noise, music, stands selling steaming food and people with food served before them on tin plates, goods wrapped in big fresh leaves. But all this is only outside, noisily shoving past. Inquisitive glances pause in passing on the activity inside, and children crowd around the door. They can always be found wherever Fitzcarraldo makes his appearance.

The "ice factory" inside works according to the principle, employed well into this century, that the reaction of various salts removes heat from water in a container. Two Indian laborers stir constantly in big circular movements with a metal pole in a vat whose outside is frosted, steaming from the cold. On a wooden pallet, several long blocks of ready-made ice are stacked. Fitzcarraldo has a block sawed into four slabs and loads them onto a little cart, where he has his ice-shaving machine.

His two curs, Gringo and Verdi, have been following him, sniffing around in all the corners. Fitzcarraldo has some friendly words to spare for them, and the dogs wag their tails.


## Belén, Several Locations

Fitzcarraldo, Wilbur, and Stan, strolling through Belén, stop here and there to sell shaved ice. Hordes of children surround them; without the children there wouldn't be anything lively down in Belén.

Life here is Amazonian, as if dozing in a coma. Women sit in their open stilt huts, endlessly delousing their children, suspended in time. Vultures perch drowsily on poles that serve to anchor the houses on floats during floods, spreading their wings like heraldic animals. They often remain motionless like this for hours. Women lean over porch railings and watch the river flow lazily by. Only the river is always in motion. The air is sultry and stifling, and people hardly move. On small charcoal grills yucca roots, green bananas, guinea pigs looking like naked rats without their skin, and fish are being barbecued, and half a cayman is roasting over a large fire. This attracts Fitzcarraldo's attention.

"I've never tried crocodile," he says, and for a coin he is served a piece on a fresh palm leaf. The meat is almost milky-white. "It tastes a little of swamp," says Fitzcarraldo.

Big piles of empty turtle shells are lying about, and there are places where you have to balance your way along fallen balsa trunks so as not to sink into the swamp. There are little shacks made of bark and braided twigs sitting on logs in the bog, outhouses that float when the water is high. The place swarms with children; they comprise two-thirds of the population down here. Often, fifteen-year-old girls are already carrying their second child as a papoose; naked children grovel with pigs in the foul mud; children play marbles. Children bear loads that are far too heavy for them. Then they stop, panting and swaying.

"Fitzcarraldo!" the children cry, and Fitzcarraldo sells shaved ice, dispensing it for coins of very little value. He has clamped a lump of ice into his machine and, turning a handle, he shaves it underneath with a kind of grater. The ice, which is more like white, loosely packed snow, drops into a glass, and Fitzcarraldo pours sweet, heavy syrup over it, a bright orange or an even gaudier bright green that quickly colors all the fluffy ice. While Fitzcarraldo struggles to keep up with the urgent demand, the juggler juggles and Wilbur dances for the children with strange, almost witchlike movements. He illustrates what the juggler performs.

Stan has a fascinating way of handling the children. With three or four little balls he can juggle entire stories, in which the balls can be sad, joyful, mischievous, or scrappy. He is a true master in his field, a born street performer who reacts to every move his little spectators make, instantly involving them in his stories. Although he speaks English to the children's Amazonian Spanish, they understand everything. He tells them the gloomy ballad of the children who leap around and swim in the river, and of the child who drowned, lured to the bottom of the river by white *bufeos,* the white freshwater dolphins, so that he might become one of them. How the dolphins sing and dance in the depths, and how they sometimes come up to dance on the surface when the moon is full.

"Say, 'I am an eagle, yes I am,' " Fitzcarraldo says to his little friend Bald Eagle, who sits on the ice grater, but the parrot just yanks out a few of his last feathers and says nothing. Business is good, that's obvious.

## *Iquitos, Brothel, Night*

Molly, with her Indian maid service, resides in one of the larger, slightly more ostentatious buildings in town, which, however, lacks the refinement of the great palaces, betraying more of its plaster and cheap paint. Still, her house does offer every stimulation for lewd fantasies, with the aid of some effectively placed potted palms, orchid plants, and concealed lights. This is no mere brothel operation; rather, Molly trains pretty young Indian girls, often forcibly captured in the jungle, to be maids in distinguished households. While this is no different from procuring mistresses for rich men, Molly considers it better than letting the girls go to ruin on the street.

Molly is serene and still has the radiance of a great lady from her days as a singer, but with the years she has gained in motherliness. Although she sometimes treats her girls with severity, she never loses her fundamental note of affection. She treats Fitzcarraldo like a big boy who has to be watched, who has to be consoled at the right moment, but who has to be allowed his freedom. Molly loves Fitzcarraldo, and Fitzcarraldo loves Molly, but they have been through so much together that they don't waste big words on it.

Molly and Fitzcarraldo are seated together at a festive dinner table, Fitz wearing his best suit, his hair kept under control with a little pomade. Several of Molly's prettiest girls are serving.

"But you have good connections with some of the very rich," says Fitzcarraldo.

"With all of them," corrects Molly.

"You should see how the children scramble for their flavored ice," says Fitzcarraldo. "The news must have gotten around. Now that, on a bigger scale . . ."

"But," says Molly, "the barons here have to want something themselves. Then they finance, then they pay any price. Zulma here, for example, has only been here nine months, and now Don Araujo has already got his eye on her, and Alfredo Borja too."

"Is that one of the Borja brothers?" asks Fitzcarraldo.

"No," says Molly, "the father, the old man. And now they're trying to outbid each other on her price, you wouldn't believe it."

"With that kind of money," says Fitzcarraldo, "I'd build myself an opera house out of blocks of ice for every performance, so for each night there'd be a huge, cool palace of ice, just for one night, and then it would melt away."

"Fitz," says Molly, "you're dreaming again."

### Gentlemen's Club, Late Afternoon

The gentlemen's club in Iquitos is located on the second floor of an elegant building on the Plaza de Armas. The rooms are arranged in such a way that they open onto a spacious veranda, extending them. Large fans disperse the cigar smoke; there are comfortable cane-backed chairs and a piano on a dais, and deals are being made. This is pure masculine society; those who meet here to gamble were made rich overnight by the rubber boom. Everything is ostentatious; one displays openly how much one has acquired, and entire fortunes change owners here in less than an hour. At one of the tables they start yelling because one of the rubber barons, who apparently has won, now beheads a whole crate of champagne bottles with one, two strokes of his machete.

Fitzcarraldo sits pushed halfway to the side at a table where six players, stubbornly drunk and stubbornly taciturn, sit playing poker. The table is covered with green velvet, and set into the rim of polished mahogany there are small bowl-like holes which are far too small to hold the huge bundles of banknotes passing across the table.

One of the players, Don Araujo, waves to the waiter and orders another glass of horsepiss. The waiter, a pure Indian who apparently doesn't know proper Spanish, says, "Sí señor, horsepiss."

For the other men at the table this seems to have been a joke practiced for a long time. They trade conspiratorial glances.

"How do you count?" asks Don Araujo, as the beer is being brought.

"One, two, three."

"And what is this called?"

"Horsepiss," says the waiter.

"Good, right," they all agree, applauding.

Fitzcarraldo takes advantage of the brief interruption to address Don Araujo. "Well, what do you think of it?" he asks.

"I'll tell you what I think," says Don Araujo rather frostily. "In the first place, you can't have any patents, because that's been written in every schoolbook for the last hundred years."

"Yes," says Fitzcarraldo, now growing a little discouraged, "but I have the experience with it, the experience is what counts . . ."

"And secondly," Don Araujo continues, "what good is ice here? To cool the rubber? To put glaciers in the jungle? Or to put the Trans-Andean Railway on sled runners, then let the brakes go, and *adios*, down into the valley?"

This scores a point. The circle of players is sneering now, trying to suppress their laughter. Fitzcarraldo starts to jump up and leave.

"No, stay," Don Araujo says, pulling him down by his sleeve. "Here, take this." He hands him a single bill from a bundle so tightly packed it looks like a brick. "Play a hand with us. Ah, this precious feeling of losing money! Ecstasy!"


## Steeple, Plaza de Armas, Sunset

In a corner of the Plaza de Armas stands the shabbily built main church of the town, made of sloppy plaster with a distorted, scarcely recognizable trace of Gothic. In the center of the plaza there is a fountain, eternally dry, with benches, lawns, and trees around it. The trees, however, are all completely leafless, their branches bare. A crowd has gathered in front of the church, staring up at the spire. We recognize Fitzcarraldo and Wilbur, who have barricaded themselves in the tower, sounding the alarm. The bell, however, sounds very thin and wan; it proclaims no fire, no war, no raging storm. It sounds more like an out-of-tune teakettle.

Fitzcarraldo violently beats the clapper of the bell while Wilbur dances like a dervish. The people stare up at them. At the church door below, four policemen led by a lieutenant are trying to force the door open, but it seems to be securely barred from inside.

And then something breathtaking happens. The sky darkens, at that moment when the sun descends below the rooftops and the jungle. From all sides the sky, still bright, darkens with raging black clouds, and now we realize what they are: gigantic flocks of black, swallow-like birds, whirling into each other and against each other in increasingly narrow, furious circles and whirlpools — unimaginable, like biblical swarms of locusts. If you look into it you are seized by vertigo. The birds circle in layers above each other, within each other, six hundred thousand birds right over the Plaza de Armas. People seek refuge in the doorways, in the open bars. And then, all of a sudden, a frontal swarm forms, crashing down toward the plaza in a frenzied funnel, like a whirlwind. At the same instant, the entire demented sky coalesces to an orderly vortex, to a whipping tail of a predator lashing down on the plaza. Six hundred thousand birds land in a single unearthly whir on the few trees in the plaza. In seconds, the trees are transformed into shapeless black clumps, not one branch visible, nothing but heaps of fluttering birds. At the edge of the plaza thousands more settle on window ledges and thin stucco strips, suddenly delineating in black on the walls of the houses designs that were hardly visible before.

Up in the tower, Wilbur has gone into ecstasies, dancing, fighting an army of six hundred thousand enemies whizzing around his head, close enough to touch. Wilbur stands in the middle of a cloud of whirring birds, flailing his arms like windmill vanes and crying, "We want the Opera!" Fitzcarraldo goes on ringing the bell with a vengeance.

*Prison, Inner Courtyard*

The prison courtyard is a cheerless square, partially roofed with corrugated tin. Vultures perch sleepily on the gable. All around are cell doors, bars reaching down to the floor. From the one open cell, the yelling and coarse singing of men is heard. We recognize Fitzcarraldo's voice. Wilbur comes stumbling out of the cell, followed by the police lieutenant and Fitzcarraldo, their arms around each other's shoulders, staggering. Fitzcarraldo is waving a whiskey bottle in his right hand.

"Compadre," he shouts, "drink up! How did you like my alarm bells! Drink!" he insists.

"To your opera!" yells the lieutenant. "He who builds an opera house must be a free man. And you, compadre, look me in the eye — where is he?" But Wilbur has already taken off.

## Belén, Fitzcarraldo's Hut

Completely knocked out by his hangover, Fitzcarraldo is lying in his hammock, still fully dressed with his boots on. He senses that someone is staring at him. As usual, he gropes with his hand for the phonograph. But he doesn't get that far, as a hand stops his halfway. Fitzcarraldo opens his eyes.

There are no children standing there, no familiar wall of bodies; not even the pig is there, his fan, the long-legged sprinter. Bronski stands before him, and it is already late afternoon.

"What's going on?" asks Fitzcarraldo.

"I am your man," says Bronski.

"You are?" says Fitzcarraldo with his head still spinning, not yet fully comprehending. "My pleasure!"

"I was there yesterday," says Bronski, "when you made your appeal for the opera from the spire. It was so beautiful the way you sounded the alarm. I am an actor. May I introduce myself: Bronski."

"Yes?" says Fitzcarraldo, slowly coming to. "What time is it, anyway? Oh, my head!"

"I arrived in Iquitos just a short time ago," says Bronski. "Buffoonery is rampant on the stages of the world. What remains for us now is the jungle. You must excuse my accent, for I haven't quite shaken off Germany yet."

Then, out of the blue, without warning, he starts reciting a Shakespearean monologue, but with such boldness, such intensity, that the first sentences take your breath away. Bronski goes into a fit, a kind of raving, while people gather below the hut. Abruptly, in the middle of a sentence, Bronski breaks off.

"That is the man," says Fitzcarraldo, "or my name isn't Fitzcarraldo."


## Molly's Brothel, Toward Evening

Molly and Fitzcarraldo seem to have been conferring together for a long time; they give the impression of being in cahoots.

"I can arrange that all right," says Molly. "I have my ways, rely on me. I'll bring my girls with me and you'll see, they'll all be there. We'll have all the rubber barons together in one spot, and I'll make sure they feel really good. And you bring Bronski and your phonograph. . . . But look at you! I won't let you out of this house looking like that."

At a sign from Molly, four pretty Indian girls grab Fitzcarraldo and drag him amid his half-hearted protests up the stairs into a chamber.

"A steam bath!" Molly calls after them. "The very finest treatment for Mr. Fitzcarraldo!"

"Help!" cries Fitzcarraldo weakly to Molly, as he disappears through a doorway above.

## Garden Party, Night

A garden party with everything that is rich and has a name. Gentlemen in tails and ladies in long evening gowns. With many of the gentlemen it is obvious that their manners are poorly studied, that only a few years ago they were nobodies, that their comportment is but a thin veneer, hiding what is, in reality, a mob of cutthroats and gangsters. Chinese lanterns illuminate a luscious tropical garden, sanded paths interspersed with lawns, fireplaces where lamb is being roasted, waiters displaying fine fat fish on big silver platters to the guests, champagne in abundance. Molly is distinctly visible with all her girls, who wear identical aprons and embroidered ribbons. The girls are carrying trays with drinks. Fitzcarraldo and Bronski are present, both wearing their best suits, looking dapper and well-groomed. They stroll with a group of billionaires, the Borja brothers and Don Araujo, through the garden.

"Everyone wants money from us," complains Alfredo Borja. "The hospital, the fire brigade, and you keep straining my ear with your opera. Where will it all end?

We can't afford everything either." He wipes his greasy face and fat neck with a silk handkerchief.

"Just take a look at this." From his pocket he pulls a thick bundle of banknotes that must weigh a pound or more. "Come here and look at this."

They stop in front of the pond, whose muddy brown surface rests peacefully within the frame of its white-washed walls. Borja throws his money into the pond, only a few feet out, and at once the water is transformed into a raging tumult, as if sea monsters were at war in it. A huge *paiche*, a species of pike almost ten feet long, as thick as a man, sucks up the bundle of money with an ugly noise. Other fish fight in frenzied greed for a share of the apparent food. Fitzcarraldo is taken aback and deeply shocked, as Alfredo Borja puts on an overbearing expression.

"You see how fast our money runs downstream," he remarks superciliously. "You must have had a similar experience yourself — a railway is bound to swallow up a lot of money. There must be something titillating about going bankrupt."

Fitzcarraldo is having difficulty maintaining his composure; we can clearly see him wrestling with his urge to throw Borja into the pool. "I have my phonograph with me, along with the very first recordings of Caruso, the ones from Milan and some later ones from New York. You only have to listen to them once, then you'll understand me. And look at this man here, Bronski."

"Ah," says Don Araujo, "this gentleman was supposed to recite something from Mr. Shakespeare. Could we start with that? You know, such a chance to meet all of one's friends and rivals in one place doesn't present itself often. Please start at once, and don't make it too long. Ladies and gentlemen, may we have your attention for a moment please!"

The party guests gather hesitantly, wrapped up in light chatter, their glasses still in their hands. Bronski begins with a monologue from *Richard III,* and after the first few sentences he works himself into such a hysterical fury that all conversation stops at once. Fear spreads through the crowd. Like a cripple, Bronski rushes toward a group of ladies who scatter in terror. He whirls around, and a gentleman behind him stops chomping his cigar. Bronski, all in a rage, with a hallucinating leer, storms toward a young girl as if having a fit, and she flees at once.

After less than two minutes, Don Araujo, evidently the host, feels forced to end the proceedings. At a signal from him, three black servants abruptly surround Bronski and hustle him out. With their white-gloved hands they touch him as if he were a leper, a reeking, mangy cur. Another servant takes Fitzcarraldo by the arm to lead him away. All hell breaks loose as Bronski tears himself away with an incredible, mad jerk and screams lines from *Richard III* into the faces of the Borjas.

"Don't worry, ladies and gentlemen, these two gentlemen are harmless, they've just had some soul-stirring experiences." Don Araujo makes a studied bow in the direction of Fitzcarraldo. "Sir, my domestics will accompany you into the kitchen. My dog's cook will prepare you a meal. Thank you very much, gentlemen, you were superb."

Bronski falls silent, he is now nothing but wrath incarnate, sparkling and glowing, pondering murder; now, in his muteness, he is one with the part.

Suddenly Fitzcarraldo, icily controlled, pulls over one of Molly's girls carrying a tray filled with champagne glasses. He grabs a glass, raises it: "To Shakespeare," he says, and drinks it in one gulp. Immediately followed by the next one. "To your dog's cook!" And then the next one: "To Verdi!" And another, and another. "To Rossini, to Caruso!"

On a sudden impulse, Don Araujo grabs the last remaining glass, raises it, and addresses the whole speechless assembly: "To Fitzcarraldo, *conquistador of the useless*. Cheers!"

Fitzcarraldo moves up, only inches away from Don Araujo's face. Don Araujo doesn't flinch. Fitzcarraldo speaks in a low voice, trembling with restraint. "As sure as I am standing here, one day I shall bring Grand Opera to Iquitos. I shall outgut you. I shall outnumber you. I shall outbillion you. I shall outrubber you. I shall outperform you."

"You pigs, you dirty pigs, you savage pigs!" Bronski screams in a voice that can no longer be called human. In an instant a fistfight with the servants breaks out. Molly, horrified by the way her friends have been treated, demonstratively departs the scene with all her girls. The whole thing ends in wild uproar, a wild melee.

## Belén, Amazon Riverbank

Vast and calm, the greatest river on earth flows by. It is raining in tranquil streams, everything is water in water. Ships draw calmly past. Thunderous clouds hang heavy in the sky. Fitzcarraldo is sitting with Wilbur and Stan in a cantina, protected by a palm roof. We see them from the rear, watching the downpour. A drunken *cauchero* lies near them on the floor, snoring. Mournfully and abstractedly Stan juggles some balls. The rain drips down from the roof in a thick curtain. There is a long silence.

"I could kill myself, the best things always occur to me later. I should have said: 'Sir, you are dead as a doornail, you're not alive anymore.' And he would have said: 'I think you are mistaken, I am still standing firm on my two legs.' And I would have said, 'When you shoot an elephant, he remains on his legs for ten days before he topples over.' And I should have, I wanted to say: 'Sir, the reality of your world is nothing more than a bad caricature of the great operas.' "

"We have to get rich with rubber ourselves," says Stan. "How did these guys do it? They didn't have anything to start with."

"First of all," says Fitzcarraldo, "you need land. It costs almost nothing around here, but all the good areas, where the trees are worthwhile, have been parceled out. And then you need a big steamboat, to make shipments up and down river and bring in provisions for large numbers of forest workers. And we don't have either."

"But," says Stan, "on the Ucayali there's still an area with millions of rubber trees, almost as big as Belgium."

"But you can't get there," says Fitzcarraldo, "it's on the upper course of the Ucayali. Farther downstream are the rapids, the Pongo das Mortes, which you'll never get past. You're not the first clever person who thought of that."

"And the Pongo das Mortes?" asks Wilbur into the ensuing pause.


## Pongo das Mortes, Early Morning

Jungle, steep mountains, steaming fog. Parrots squawk, the water roars like wild bulls. The river below the narrow part of the Pongo das Mortes widens quickly to half a kilometer, but we can see distinctly that further up the Pongo the cliffs start rising up vertically. Higher up they are overgrown with dense jungle. It is high water, yellowish-brown as it surges along. Fitzcarraldo is standing at the water's edge in the dense jungle, with Don Aquilino at his side, a fine-boned man who looks like a Spanish aristocrat. Deeper inside the forest, a few ragged Indians with machetes stand staring out over the water.

"And your territory?" asks Fitzcarraldo.

"It ends right here where the Pongo empties. Downstream it reaches for thirty kilometers."

"And beyond the Pongo?" Fitzcarraldo asks.

"Well, beyond . . ." Don Aquilino sighs. "I would like to be there myself. If you are good at climbing, and over the mountains at that, then good luck to you. We've thought about building a road across it, but it would be a crazy venture, and then there'd still be something missing."

"A boat," muses Fitzcarraldo, finishing the thought out loud. "And through the Pongo by boat — nobody's ever tried it?"

"Want to see for yourself?" asks Don Aquilino. "You have to see it with your own eyes, or you'll never believe me."

## In the Pongo das Mortes, Boat Trip

We are with Fitzcarraldo and Don Aquilino on a powerful motorboat, steered by an Indian boatman. All three are wearing life vests. To the left and right, rocky walls vanish up into the fog. The rushing water forms huge whirlpools which, like whirlwinds with a deep hole in the center, often drift in semicircles against the current.

"What's that?" asks Fitzcarraldo, frightened.

"Shh, quiet, don't talk," the boatman calls in his native tongue.

"What's he saying?" Fitzcarraldo asks.

"You must be quiet," says Don Aquilino. "Whoever talks or makes noise will be swallowed up by the whirlpools. That's what the Indians here believe."

The current becomes so violent, and the waves farther upstream tower above them so threateningly that the boat must be tied to big boulders on the riverbank. Here we can see ground-up pieces of tree trunks lying around, torn and filed smooth by the water into weird shapes.

"In flood season the water rises more than thirty feet above this level," says Don Aquilino. "Take a look at these marks." And indeed, things don't look so good; we can sense violent forces here. "We can go a bit farther on foot."


## Riverbank in the Pongo das Mortes

Fitzcarraldo and Don Aquilino have penetrated deeper into the Pongo on foot, up to the point where they cannot proceed any farther because the rocky walls plunge almost vertically down into the raging torrent. We are in the midst of the most furious rapids in the whole of South America, a *pure inferno*. We see Don Aquilino drawing Fitzcarraldo's ear toward him, shouting over the roar.

"The Indians call the rapids *chirimagua*, 'the angry spirits.' Anyone who falls in there is done for. The Indians also say, 'The water has no hair to hold on to,' " he shouts, laughing.

We see him and Fitzcarraldo, their life vests still tied around them, as they seek a firm hold on the slippery rock. Far above them the sky is veiled by fog. The rocky walls are lost in it. Colibri hummingbirds dive down out of the roiling fog. Lianas hang out of the nothingness, almost reaching the seething of hell. There is no passage through here, never.


## Jungle Path

The jungle is dusky and moldering, foul vapors of organic decay rise from the ground. Rain streams down incessantly, and incessantly the monkeys scream their wailing noises in the treetops. Shrill sounds of birds in the liana thickets, an enormous, mysterious orchestra reaches out to the edges of the world.

A path, hardly visible to the naked eye, winds its way through dripping green profusion. We notice it only when a strange procession, led by a half-naked Indian, passes by at a lope. The Indian has something resembling a miner's lamp attached to his headband, and in his right hand he has a machete, sharp as a razor, which he wields with surprisingly lithe, swinging movements to hack through the constantly creeping foliage and lianas. Behind him hastens Don Aquilino in a grotesque-looking hat hung with a mosquito net, tied at his neck, making him look like a beekeeper. Behind him follows Fitzcarraldo, stumbling, slipping, and beating about with his hands to ward off the mosquitoes. After him come some Indians with closely-cropped hair, barefoot and half naked. Shy and soundless they glide through the sinister forest.

Don Aquilino turns to Fitzcarraldo and says, "I told you this wasn't a joyride." Fitzcarraldo falls into the muddy, putrid, rain-soaked soil but is back on his feet at once, hurrying on bravely. The jungle swallows up the men.

## Jungle, Rubber Tree

The men have stopped at a rubber tree.

"So that's a rubber tree?" Fitzcarraldo asks, disappointed by such a small, stupid, ordinary-looking tree with its gray bark.

"Right. *Hevea brasiliensis*," says Don Aquilino.

The Indian with the lamp on his head carves a kind of fishbone pattern into the bark with quick, practiced movements, sticking a little wooden peg into it, angled downward, as a viscous, whitish juice immediately begins to ooze out of the cuts and flow together. The milky juice is channeled precisely to the wooden tap, from which it drips down into a tin can that one of the Indians has hurriedly fastened to the trunk with a wire. The Indian speaks Jívaro, and Don Aquilino interprets.

"The word for rubber comes from their language, they call the tree *cautchou,* 'the tree that weeps.' These bare-asses here are very fond of flowery language; gold they call 'sweat of the sun,' and bees 'fathers of honey.' It's no easy job disciplining these bare-asses. That's why each one is given his own separate area, and as the trees are pretty far apart, it's quite a runaround. But that's the only way to keep them from making mischief."

## Jungle, Settlement of the Rubber-Gatherers

In the middle of the dripping jungle is a small clearing, where some sad hens stand in the dripping rain. They stand apathetically, completely motionless, thinking intensely about nothing. Parrots fill the treetops with noise, rain gushes down, far away a mighty thunderclap rumbles. Moisture steams up between the tree trunks. A few very primitive huts are scattered about. In the center of the clearing are two protective palm-roofs of differing height, erected almost vertically. On the ground between the two lean-tos, a fire is flickering, and over it a wooden pole fixed in a forked branch is being rotated. On the pole a wild growth of brownish rubber has already collected.

One Indian turns the pole as another carefully pours on the milky rubber juice which, because of the smoking fire, coagulates quickly into a thin skin, making the ball thicker. Corrosive white smoke rises against the rain and lingers in the clearing and among the trees, refusing to disperse. Fitzcarraldo huddles under the steep lean-to with Don Aquilino, trying to avoid the smoke by keeping his head down. In his hand he holds a cigarette, swollen by the humidity, and he approaches the blaze rolling it between his thumb and middle finger to dry it. It is getting too hot for him, and the cigarette is still swollen with dampness. The Indians work silently.

"You are a strange bird," says Don Aquilino, "but somehow I like you."

"I'll tell you something," Fitzcarraldo says. "There was a funny little Frenchman, at the time when North America was hardly explored, one of those very early trappers. From Montreal he went west, and he was the first white man to set eyes on Niagara Falls. When he returned, he told of waterfalls that were more vast and immense than people had ever dreamed of. No one believed him, they thought he was a madman or a liar. But he was a visionary. They asked him, 'What is your proof?' and he answered, 'My proof is that I've seen the falls.'"

Fitzcarraldo tries to light his cigarette with a glowing twig, but it refuses to catch fire. "Excuse me for having told you this now," he says, coughing. "I don't really know myself what it's all got to do with me."

The camp is wrapped in mythical vapors, and the rain presses upon the sad forest with the full colossal weight of an entire continent. A grandiose music emerges. We breathe deeply.

## Don Aquilino's House, Night

A broad veranda, built on poles like the rest of this stately house of Don Aquilino's. It is lit by kerosene lamps. From one of the rooms, the door of which is ajar, a strip of light spills out. A man crosses the light, casting a fleeting shadow on the floor of the veranda. Only now do we realize that several Indian women and girls are huddled in the darkness between the braided-cane chairs on the veranda. Steadily the rain drums its song on the rippled tin roof of the house.

The living room, seen through the door of the veranda. Simple furniture, the quarters of a pioneer, with only a massive mahogany desk to suggest that Don Aquilino is one of the very rich people in this country. A young Indian woman whisks in from outside carrying two glasses of thick, rich papaya juice. Fitzcarraldo reaches absent-mindedly for a glass. He is not really paying attention to Don Aquilino, who is talking to him.

"Women, that's the only pleasant part of this business out here, there are enough of them. Unfortunately, for the first two or three years you've got to be out here sweating in it, or else everything goes cockeyed."

But Fitzcarraldo cannot tear his gaze from a map hanging on the wall. It attracts him magically. Don Aquilino steps up beside him.

"This, here, from the Pongo to where the Ucayali empties into the Amazon, is my area," he says. "And this here is Araujo's territory, as big as Switzerland. And this here, Alejandro Borja's, and this Gustavo Borja's, and this over here, Clodomiro Borja's. And up north of them, Hardenburg's, you know, the only Prussian. Farther east you see the Peruvian Amazon Company, that's a joint-stock company." He points to all these places on the map with cursory, magnanimous gestures appropriate for a landowner of his caliber. Only one big gap remains — beyond the Pongo, up the Ucayali River.

Closer to the map, we see a sector of the Amazon region with several tributaries branching out, which, in the Peruvian Andes, curve south into parallel mountain valleys, while in the Andes of Ecuador and Colombia they behave similarly, except that they all branch out to the north. The Pongo das Mortes lies between the last heights of the Peruvian Andes. The adjacent river parallel to the Ucayali is the Pachitea, which sometimes runs as far as one hundred kilometers distant, but in some places comes quite close. On the whole, however, one gets the impression that the two run approximately parallel to each other. The Pachitea feeds into the Amazon River above Iquitos, the Ucayali a little farther downstream from Iquitos. On almost all the other tributaries, gridded spaces of vast dimensions have been marked off, apparently the territories of the rubber barons indicated by Don Aquilino. On the upper course of the Ucayali, that is to say, beyond the Pongo, an ungridded rectangle has been marked, and on the Pachitea there is nothing at all.

"What does that square mean?" Fitzcarraldo wants to know.

"Well," says Don Aquilino, "that's the rubber region óf the Ucayali, with about fourteen million trees, and look, it's the only one that has yet to find an owner. You'd have to be able to fly."

"That's been done already," says Fitzcarraldo. "And what's up there on the Pachitea? Why is there nothing marked there?"

"There are no rubber trees there, that is to say, there are a few, but it wouldn't be worthwhile," says Don Aquilino. "The only thing you'll find there are savage Indians. White civilization stopped short at their doorstep because it wouldn't have been profitable for us."

An idea akin to madness has suddenly seized Fitzcarraldo. He stares along the Pachitea, and then he stares along the Ucayali. A sudden flash of inspiration shoots through his mind, but he doesn't want to give himself away. He grabs Don Aquilino's glass by mistake and drinks it down, trying to overcome his hoarseness, but he barely manages.

"How exact is this map? Is there anything more exact?" he blurts out.

"Yes," says Don Aquilino, "why?"

Fitzcarraldo just stares at him glassy-eyed.

"In 1896 a group of surveyors got to the upper Pachitea, along with some soldiers, and some of them were murdered. Then the Jesuits penetrated a bit farther up the river. They have their last outpost in Saramiriza, and from then on it's only Jívaros. Savages — you know what I mean? They make shrunken heads. Have you ever seen one?"

"Yes," says Fitzcarraldo. "I mean no . . . sort of."

Don Aquilino withdraws briefly to an adjoining room, returning with a shrunken head smaller than a fist, discolored and almost black. It is the head of an Indian with long hair. The lips have been sewn together with a fuzzy thread.

"Genuine Jívaro, from this region here, but this one is from twenty years ago," says Don Aquilino. But Fitzcarraldo is unable to pay attention because a *great idea* has taken hold of him.


## Iquitos, Molly's Brothel, Day

A restlessness seizes events from now on, something urgent and insistent. Incidents crowd each other and pick up tempo.

Molly is busy assigning one of her girls to a fat, rich client. He has narrowed it down to four of the young Indian girls, and the others are presently leaving the room.

"So this is your final selection," says Molly, very businesslike.

"I guess so," sighs the man, "now it's getting complicated."

Fitzcarraldo bursts in and pulls the amazed Molly to one side; she hasn't seen him like this for a long time.

"I think I'll take all four," the man says, half apologetically, half like an accomplice.

"Molly, you have to stake me — every red cent you can spare," Fitzcarraldo blurts out. "You won't believe it."

"Oh God, not again," says Molly.

His voice becomes low, threateningly determined. "I have a great *idea,*" says Fitzcarraldo, spreading out maps, showing detailed sectors from some of the tributaries of the Amazon, on the nearest table.


## Molly's Bedroom, Night

Molly's bedroom is dominated by a huge, stylish brass bed from France; otherwise only a few indoor plants catch the eye, and a night table with expensive perfumes in cut-crystal bottles. Molly and Fitzcarraldo lie in bed, pleasantly tired and a little rumpled, but Fitzcarraldo is in a terrifically good mood, with Molly weary but loving by his side.

"First I have to see the notary and then I must get a boat, it has to be called Molly and then . . ."

"But," says Molly, "for a really big boat even my money isn't enough."

Fitzcarraldo has no answer to this at the moment, but he is happy that he has got around Molly once again. He grabs under the sheet that covers the two of them, poking around near his knee. Molly wonders what he's doing, until Fitzcarraldo suddenly produces a cockroach, an enormous specimen bigger than any we've ever seen. Fitzcarraldo lets go of the kicking monster, and it scuttles across the sheet in a mad sprint and disappears onto the floor.

"We'll have children yet," says Fitzcarraldo, thinking himself witty.


## Notary's Office

The notary's office has everything that made turn-of-the-century Peruvian bureaus unpleasant. Scrubbed, joyless wooden floors, racks stuffed with files in which nothing can ever be found, an ugly photo of the reigning president, a dusty flag in a stand, and a desk that tries to be impressive but is merely repulsive. In a corner a couple of minor clerks are working on some papers, and even at this distance their incompetence is obvious. The notary is a gaunt, elderly, very tall man who is sitting behind his desk, slightly stooped in order not to tower above it too much. In front of him is a map with surveyor's markings, a fully completed contract, and various other forms that have to be signed. Fitzcarraldo and Wilbur sit opposite him. Fitzcarraldo seems self-assured, and Wilbur, who wants to imitate him but overdoes it, assumes an expression that is the picture of self-confidence. Fitzcarraldo has a bundle of money lying on the table in front of him, still keeping his hand on it.

The notary straightens up a little more in his chair. "You must sign with your full, given name; pseudonyms like yours are not permissible here, I'm afraid. Now the procedure. The acquisition process goes step by step: you and your partner sign first, then you hand over the money, and I complete the document with my signature. But before you do this, I must direct your attention to the option clause. The Peruvian government requires, through its legislative bodies, that a region of this size shall have been taken into possession by proof and by deed within nine months' time, and that the first operational steps to exploit said region be undertaken, or else your rights of exploitation terminate with no compensation. The government is concerned that said areas be developed competently and speedily, so that they do not go to waste."

"Just hand it over," says Fitzcarraldo.

"We knew all that anyway," echoes Wilbur.

"Allow me one question of a personal nature," says the notary. "Do you really know what you're doing?"

"We're going to be billionaires," says Fitzcarraldo.

The notary's gaze passes slowly from one to the other. Evidently he is dealing not with an idiot, but with an idiot and a madman as well.

"Well?" says Wilbur.

"Go on, sign," says Fitzcarraldo.

## Río Itaya, Tributary

A fine, sad rain envelops river and forest. The yellowish-brown Itaya flows lazily. An arm branches off to the side, with grey-black muddy banks and equally muddy sandbars. The hull of a completely rusted ship lies there in the mud half-broken, with no housing on it anymore, no engine, the ship having no value even as scrap metal. With Wilbur's aid, Fitzcarraldo poles his *peke-peke* in shallow water right up to the wreck. But he knows already, and we can tell by his movements, that there's no sense in it. "No," he says, "that's not it."

## Jungle Near Puerto Maldonado

It is raining even harder, a thunderstorm emptying itself out over the jungle, rushing with a low steady sound down through the silent giants of the trees. Fitzcarraldo and Wilbur are standing in mud up to their ankles, covering themselves with large banana leaves which they hold over their heads. They are peering straight ahead from beneath the dripping curtain.

We see what they see. In the middle of the forest, far away from the course of the Madre de Dios, a paddle-wheel steamboat of mammoth proportions lies stuck in the jungle, no doubt deposited by an enormous flood more than a decade ago. Lianas have slung themselves around it and made it grow into one with the giant trees. Out of the belly of the gaping hulk a tree has grown at least thirty feet tall. Fresh, proliferous greenery covers the deck and spills out of the captain's cabin. A weird, mysterious sight, as if grown from the gloomy dreams of the jungle itself.

Fitzcarraldo stands there and stares. "No," he says, and turns around. With heavy steps, sloshing in the mud, he goes away.


## Río Nanay

Fitzcarraldo and Wilbur, they stand and stare. Clouds are towering behind them, white like fluffy cotton. The sun is shining. Fitzcarraldo wears a sheepish face, and Wilbur smiles like an acolyte during mass, a smile of religious trance. Fitzcarraldo removes his hat and holds it against his chest.

"Wilbur," he says solemnly, "that's it."

We see what the two see. There it lies, *the ship*, the Nariño, the jewel, pulled carelessly onto land, covered all over with rust and showing some gaping holes below the water line, yet sad, beautiful, and *inviting*. The Nariño measures 120 feet, has cabins on two levels and, on top of the second, the bridge, several lifeboats, and a smoke-stack sticking up at an angle. Added to this are masts fore and aft. It is no paddlewheel steamer, which are very rare in these waters anyway, but originally had a screw propeller that is gone now, and we can still see the driveshaft leading into the interior. The rudder has broken off, the cabins on deck have only traces of white paint, and grass is growing along some of the edges. But the ship looks good enough to fall in love with; yes, at last, that's it.

We accompany Wilbur and Fitzcarraldo on an exploration through the boat, poking around with them in the cabins and the engine room. Nearby, almost surrounding the bow of the boat, there are some log huts on poles, and from the windows children and mestizo women stare over at them in sleepy indifference. The engine, a big, old steam engine, is still there, but evidently it no longer runs and hasn't in years. On deck there are magnificent ornaments and fittings of brass, and the upper frames of the cabins are decorated with beautiful ornamental molding from which the paint is peeling away. In the cabins, which are somewhat cramped, there are bunk beds, although only their fancifully decorated metal frames remain. The galley is still almost fully equipped; there are even pots and spoons left. Fitzcarraldo is excited, and Wilbur runs around the decks, faster and faster, disappears into a cabin, then comes shooting out again from a different place. He falls into steps that are more like a strange dance. At the helm, a balding chicken broods. Screeching, it leaves its roost.

## Office of the Borja Brothers

The three Borja brothers, looking like Mafia bosses in elegant tropical suits, offer Fitzcarraldo a cigar. All four men in the room light thick, black Brazilian cigars; all business has been concluded, all papers signed, the money delivered. The three brothers show a feigned curiosity.

"One thing," says Clodomiro Borja, enveloping himself in a thick cloud of smoke, "one thing interests us, of course" — he asks this question with slow, savoring pleasure — "you are not by any chance thinking of a connecting link for your railway?"

"Yes," Gustavo Borja pretends in a servile tone, "a kind of traffic connection by boat from the Atlantic, up the Amazon, and from there across the Andes by train to the Pacific coast? Do correct us if we are wrong."

Fitzcarraldo veils himself in smoke and silence.

"Or do you intend to brave the Pongo in the Nariño? Bold! Excellent! You know, the three of us have a bet going, how long it will take until you are bankrupt again. Don't take it personally, please, we are all sportsmen, aren't we?"

"No, there is only one of us," says Fitzcarraldo. "I shall move a mountain. Good day."

## Río Nanay, Where the Nariño Lies

The place seems transformed, there is enormous activity around the boat and on deck. At least a hundred people are busily working. Scaffolding has been erected along the sides of the ship. There the rusty metal plates are being torn down. On deck there is sawing and planing. There is hammering and forging, shouting and singing. It is delightful to watch. Many of the workers are children, carrying things or painting. Fitzcarraldo is in constant motion, rushing about giving instructions, directing the carpenters as they hammer and saw. He crawls into the engine room, where the engine and boiler are being taken apart.

On deck, Wilbur is sweeping with glowing enthusiasm. Stan sustains the children's mood by way of speedily conjured tricks with a few balls. Bronski rushes like a raving fury into a group of men who are obviously about to fasten a metal plate to precisely the wrong spot on the hull. Anyone would be scared by him. Beside the ship a small carpenter's workshop has been set up in the open air, and next to it an improvised forge, with a furnace kept glowing by some children with a big bellows.

We become aware of something fascinating: at that time welding was unknown, so all metal plates were fastened with rivets. The rivets are heated red-hot, and a human chain of rivet-throwers brings the rivets with terrific speed and agility to the places where the rivets are required at the moment, often inaccessible spots inside the hull where the last riveter lies in a twisted position, catching the glowing rivet in an asbestos glove, then fitting it into the right place. Small fires are glimmering, where women cook fish and yucca on improvised grills, pots of fish soup are simmering, hens are being plucked, and little children crawl in the mud.

We observe Stan closely, how he makes four balls dance. Children climb around him on the pipework on deck, scraping and brushing the rust off. Stan speaks in the rhythm of the balls; finally he drops one. "I just wonder," says Stan, "what he . . . actually . . . plans . . . to do . . . damn, I've lost one."


## Foundry, Iquitos

Into the clay ground a smelting oven of the most primitive kind has been set like a frayed iron volcano; bellows make the fire in the earth white-hot. The foundry looks more like a forge of the bronze age than a modern construction. The plant is covered by a roof of corrugated tin set on poles. Near the foundry a workman is fashioning a clay mold; we see that it will be a large propeller. With a trowel he gives the last corrective touches to the contour. Half-naked, sweating workers stand around; Fitzcarraldo is among them. Foundry pots lie about, fastened to metal poles for carrying. Pigs grunt in a fermenting garbage heap, ducks waddle around amid pieces of metal. In a corner a pig is slaughtered, women nurse babies, and a dwarfish, crippled woman works at a sewing machine. The leaves of a papaya tree hang into the chaotic yard. The bronze mixture, meanwhile, is boiling white; workers grab a foundry pot filled with sloshing, hissing, white liquid metal and pour it into the mold. There is a malevolent seething, steaming, and hissing as the propeller is formed.

## Little Shipyard, Iquitos

A small shipyard housed in temporary shelters has been installed upstream, as primitive and chaotic as the foundry. Frightfully huge tree trunks are being lifted out of the water onto land by a crane. Workers peel off the bark with gigantic crowbars. At the river a chaos of boats and people; ships ride the current up and downstream; vultures, sluggish with satiation, are shooed off, landing again on the same piece of stinking carrion. In the shipyard Indian carpenters work on two of the Nariño's lifeboats, keels and rudder shafts jutting like skeletons into the sky. Piles of lumber, planed planks, fireplaces, smoking pitch for caulking. In their midst an elderly mestizo works on a life-sized carving, the figurehead of the Nariño. Already we can clearly distinguish a girl's body, with naked breasts and Indian features; a thick anaconda coils itself around her body and disappears behind her back, emerging below her left breast. A flat river turtle creeping toward her belly covers her sex.

Fitzcarraldo is talking to the woodcarver, who does not stop working. "When is the señorita going to be ready?" he wants to know, and we can see that he would like to hurry him.

"*La señorita?*" the woodcarver says. "*Mañana!*"

"Tomorrow, tomorrow," Fitzcarraldo says half angry, half resigned, "for ten days you've been saying *mañana* to me. The launching is in four days, and you keep saying *mañana*. I'ts enough to drive a man mad!"


## Outside Iquitos Bar

In front of one of the cheap bars, two to three hundred people are crowded far out into the street, all barefoot, in torn trousers, impoverished, disillusioned, destroyed by their life in the jungle. Disease, alcohol, and hopelessness have left their mark on their appearance. Near them, piled directly along the edge of the street, bales of rubber lie ready for shipping. A tall, crude, two-wheeled cart, to which a pair of zebu oxen is hitched, stands there, and a drunk sleeping on the loading platform is snoring loudly. Pushing at the door, shoving for position, everyone wants to enter the bar at once.

## Inside Bar

Behind two tables pulled together, Stan, Wilbur, Fitzcarraldo, and Bronski are seated like a tribunal. Bronski cannot stay in his seat any longer. He jumps up and attacks the chaotic throng being shoved in from outside. He shouts in a cracking voice and actually succeeds in spreading so much terror and fright around him that, momentarily, something like order is created. Beside the tables stands a tall, quiet, rather heavy man with deep-set eyes, a little embarrassed: Jaime de Aguila. Fitzcarraldo leans back contentedly in his armchair.

"We've already got the most important man," he says. "Tell me, do you really speak Jívaro?"

"I lived fourteen years with the Jívaros," Jaime says curtly, leaving no doubt.

"You have been sailing the rivers safely so far?" asks Fitzcarraldo.

"Yes, my last ship was the Adolfo," says Jaime, "but I've been out of commission for a couple of years. My eyesight isn't so good anymore, but I can't be tricked."

"What do you mean?" asks Fitzcarraldo.

"The jungle plays tricks on your senses. It's full of lies, dreams, illusions. I have learned to tell the difference," says Jaime.

"And you took part in the Pachitea expedition in '96?"

"Yes," says Jaime, "as helmsman. On the way back I was the captain. The captain died, there were only five survivors."

Fitzcarraldo stands up and extends his hand to him in a firm grip. "Jaime de Aguila," he says a little solemnly, "you now have full captain's authority."

Jaime returns the handshake wordlessly, and he radiates great confidence.

A small, wiry man pushes his way forward, an American who somehow has stumbled into these parts, able to recite poems, who had heard they were looking for people for the opera, the great theater. And before Fitzcarraldo can stop him, he begins reciting a poem, faltering and pathetic. Bronski turns green, sickened by the ghastly recital, which Fitzcarraldo manages to interrupt at last.

"We need people for the Nariño! What can you do?"

"I know something about engines," the man says, surprised.

"Keep in touch," says Fitzcarraldo curtly.


## Outside Iquitos Bar, Evening

There are no longer so many people in front of the bar, the rows have thinned out. But there is still a good deal of pushing going on. With a slightly swaying step, barefoot and wearing only linen pants and a straw hat, a somewhat pot-bellied man comes plowing his way through the crowd with great self-assurance.

68

## Inside Bar

The selection committee is still sitting, as before, except that now Jaime de Aguila is sitting at the table with them, evidently exercising his rights, doing so with a completely natural authority. The man in the straw hat plants himself before Fitzcarraldo.

"Hola, brethren," he says, "I am Huerequeque. I am your man."

Fitzcarraldo turns to Jaime de Aguila, who, before he can ask his question, gives a short gesture indicating: no.

"Compadre," says Huerequeque, whose attention the signal did not escape, "I am the best cook in the Amazon, I have been on every boat and, amigo," he whispers softly, his eyes growing even smaller and slyer than before, his expression even more audacious, "I know what you are planning. I'm no blockhead. Now and then Huerequeque may spill one too many into his gills, but up here," he says, pointing to his temples, "it's electric. *Eléctrico!* I am the best gunman up and down the entire Amazon."

This remark makes Fitzcarraldo prick up his ears; he glances toward Jaime, who, in spite of himself, nods in agreement.

"I took part in the Chaco wars," Huerequeque says. "I was at the upper Napo when we had a hell of a fight with the bare-asses. Amigo, I am Huerequeque."

Fitzcarraldo realizes that this man has thought further ahead than all the others, and he doesn't want the conversation to continue in this vein. "Huerequeque, you are our cook."

## Iquitos, Hardware Store

A big hardware store, in the typical chaos of all the shops and stores in this town, with rolls of wire lying around, kegs of nails, tools, cable drums, steel girders, corrugated tin. The owner of the shop, a small, bald Jew, scurries about and shoos a couple of helpers into the back room. Fitzcarraldo and Jaime de Aguila are inside and hand the merchant a list, which they check against their own copy.

"Machetes," says the merchant.

"Two hundred," Fitzcarraldo says.

"Two hundred and fifty," says Jaime.

"Okay, two hundred and fifty," says Fitzcarraldo.

"Steel girders: two inches thick, one and a half inches, and one inch," says the merchant.

"Everything you've got," says Fitzcarraldo.

"Everything?" the merchant asks, more and more convinced that he is dealing with a madman.

"Everything. Everything you've got. Cog wheels, crowbars, saws, winches: everything you have in stock," says Fitzcarraldo firmly. "Do you have train rails?"

"*Rails?*" says the merchant, sweat beading on his brow. "What? How? We don't carry those. Your railroad, are you really going to . . ."

"No, we aren't," says Fitzcarraldo, "but never mind, if you don't have any in stock."

## Belén Market

Fitzcarraldo and Jaime de Aguila are plowing their way through the teeming Belén marketplace, followed by Indian porters who, heavily loaded already, are carrying their loads on their backs with the aid of head straps. Jaime has apparently taken on the responsibility of buying provisions. They stop at a stall overflowing with black tobacco; several women are busy rolling primitive cigarettes with quick, practiced movements, almost like a small factory. Jaime gives some brief instructions in Spanish. The women pack the entire contents of the stall in two big bags.

"All of it?" asks Fitzcarraldo, astonished.

"Yes," says Jaime, "we need tobacco. Now we only need guns, hammocks, and kerosene for the lamps."

The two of them stop at another stall, where in tin canisters a sticky black substance is for sale. The canisters are handled with the utmost care, as though there were high explosives inside. Some of the gooey, pitch-like material is oozing out from under the lids. The Indian merchant touches the canisters with special respect.

"This is going to be pretty expensive," says Jaime.

"What do we need curare for, actually, and why twenty kilos all at once?" Fitzcarraldo asks, surprised. "A milligram scratched into the skin is enough to kill a pig, after all."

But Jaime is sure of himself, he is a man with inestimable experience. "The Jívaros," he says, "are a tribe that uses the poison arrow. Not knowing how to make the poison themselves, they trade with neighboring tribes for it."

The Indian joins in, and for the first time we hear the Jívaro dialect.

"What does he say?" asks Fitzcarraldo.

"He says," Jaime translates, "for a knife-point full of gold dust you get a white woman in the brothel here for one night, but for a teaspoonful of this here you get a Jívaro woman for a week."


*Iquitos, Riverbank at the Amazon*

A holiday. There it lies in its moorings, the Nariño, in a festive place cleared of the host of other boats: truly a glorious craft, beautiful enough to fall in love with. The decks have been rebuilt, the cabins gleam white with their fresh coat of enamel, the hull looks completely new, mended so perfectly and painted gleaming white, garlands adorn her. *La Señorita,* the lasciviously sensual figurehead, looms upward from the bow. Some ten thousand happy, curious people have gathered at the steep riverbank, high up on the edge of the city. A brass band is playing loud and off-key, peddlers sell sweets and fried things wrapped in leaves, there are children in countless numbers; it is a big day. A zebu cow is heaved aboard with a crane.

On deck the crew has assembled, lined up in formation, among them some pretty tough-looking characters, the wildest to be found in the entire Amazon region.

Jaime, the captain, proudly wears a gold-braided captain's uniform and looks like a Spanish grandee. Huerequeque arrives late, driving two young, very pretty Indian girls before him up the gangway.

"I won't have those women on my ship," Jaime shouts down from the bridge.

"Compadre," Huerequeque shouts back, "I need them in the galley, they are my assistants. I can't cook without them." By this time they are already on board. In the general festivity this incident is quickly forgotten.

Ashore, Fitzcarraldo stands there in his white linen suit as proud as a king, with Molly by his side, wearing her finest, most elegant dress and a big Parisian hat. She looks particularly beautiful and radiant, a grand lady amid a throng of barefoot, shouting people. Fitzcarraldo holds a rope in his hand that leads to the bow of the boat, which is partly veiled.

"Molly," he cries, "you'll be an opera singer again. You'll make your big entrance. This is your day!" He kisses her freely and impetuously in front of all the people and pulls the rope. The cloth drops off the bow to reveal the new name of the ship. *Molly Aida* is emblazoned on it in shimmering, decorative golden letters.

"Oh, Fitz," says Molly, "that's more than my poor weak heart can stand. I know it."

"Right, and now comes the highly official part," says Fitzcarraldo proudly. "We couldn't do a real launching at the Nanay, it was too shallow out there. We had to drag the *Molly* into the water with a tugboat." He hands Molly a small champagne bottle that hangs from a rope tied to the bow. "Hard!" says Fitzcarraldo.

Molly swings the bottle against the side of the boat, where it shatters, foaming. All of a sudden she begins to cry out loud. Fitzcarraldo hugs her to him. Cheers ring out. Jaime toots the big foghorn, and the brass band plays. Gringo and Verdi remain on the shore, wagging their tails.

We see the *Molly Aida* shove off from the riverbank, smoke pouring out of the chimney. People wave, some toss their hats in the air. Yes, Fitzcarraldo has friends. The *Molly Aida* picks up speed and heads upstream. The cheering dies down, the people stare in disbelief.

On the riverbank we see Molly. Shouts are heard. "Wherever is he going? He's going upstream!"

The three Borja brothers step up to Molly in incredulous astonishment. "He's not going to the Ucayali River. He should be heading downstream," says Clodomiro Borja.

Molly suddenly stops weeping; pride surges up in her. "Yes," she says, "you have seen right. Brian Sweeney Fitzgerald is moving against the Amazon!"

We see Fitzcarraldo on deck with his most faithful comrades, Wilbur and Stan. They wave back.

Iquitos, with its houses and thousands of people, shrinks to a single line. Like a lake the river widens between the town and the ship.

## Amazon River

Violently, a distant thunderstorm is building up over the vast river. Lightning flashes far away across the sky, so far that the thunder rolls but softly from horizon to horizon. In heavy, hanging streaks, a dark gush of rain pours down over the endless forest. The boat has set its course toward the horizon, and our hearts become lighter.

On deck, many of the crew have stretched out in their hammocks to get some sleep. All is quiet. The vessel is stuffed with equipment, cables, provisions. Fitzcarraldo's ice machine is lashed securely to the upper deck, and up on top, on a specially built platform, sits the phonograph. Fitzcarraldo is just covering it from the first solitary raindrops.

Wilbur is asleep in his barber chair, which he has unfolded almost horizontally — the sleep of the just, his mouth wide open. The steam engine throbs evenly, reassuringly, and the decks vibrate slightly. Jaime de Aguila stands solid, sure, and calm, steering the boat. In front of him, the parrot Bald Eagle is preening what is left of his feathers. From the galley door one of the Indian girls emerges with a basket of tropical fruit and giggles. A hand stuck under her skirt still has hold of her. When she frees herself, a man takes a step out of the galley — it is Huerequeque. *"Ay, que rico!"* he says with a gleam in his eye.

Jaime de Aguila is leaning against the railing of the bridge, alert, his head tilted at a strange angle. Fitzcarraldo has taken over the rudder.

"Starboard!" shouts Jaime. "Further starboard, we're approaching shallow water. There must be a sandbank there."

"I can't see a sandbank," says Fitzcarraldo. "How do you know there's a sandbank coming?"

"Shallow water," says Jaime, "sounds different than deep water."


## Jungle Railroad Station, Toward Evening

The boat glides softly along a narrower leg of the wide-branching river, toward the railway station landing. No other boats are tied up there, as it seems to be one of the deserted connecting links on the upper course of the Amazon, with all the sadness, desolation, and somnolence characteristic of places like this. The station lies there dead and abandoned; only a few yards back begins the jungle. A ramp with tracks slants directly down into the water, and further up, on solid ground, is the main building with its corrugated tin roof. *Trans-Andean Railways* is written there in big, rusty letters. Part of the roof has torn loose, and shreds of tin rattle malevolently, dangling in the light evening breeze. The station house gives an even greater sense of desolation due to the iron parts scattered around it, and a deserted forge and mechanic's workshop nearby. Behind it we see the stationmaster's hut and the smokestack of a locomotive.

The stationmaster, a gray-haired, seedy man in his official uniform — which he evidently has rarely worn, and which looks newly ironed with its brass buttons all polished — is standing with his Indian wife and several grimy, half-naked children in a row. Beneath his uniform jacket he is wearing no shirt; he must have just slipped on his uniform hastily, and his bare feet protrude from his trousers. From his splayed, powerful toes we can tell that he hasn't worn shoes for years. He is standing at attention, giving a half-military salute, in order to control his emotion. "Fitzcarraldo is here! At last! With a ship!"

Fitzcarraldo is the first to jump onto land, and returns the salute. The stationmaster, struggling for self-control, delivers some sort of official report, but then it all comes pouring out of him, all the things that have been piling up throughout the years of desperate waiting. As Fitzcarraldo, followed by his crew, mounts the ramp to the railway with the stationmaster, the latter starts talking like a waterfall.

"I knew you'd come back one day," he says, "I've been here six years now without salary, the station is ready for action, just look at the children; I've taken an Indian wife, the locomotive is still in good shape, although I must admit I was forced to sell a few iron parts, but those were all parts of no great importance, it's still running, this steam engine, you know, there's no iron anywhere around here, and the Indians need it for their machetes and things, I had to do it, for I had been forgotten at this post. Oh, am I glad you're here! When will you resume construction?"

Fitzcarraldo is embarrassed and silent. "You know," he says, "we had some financial problems. But we haven't completely given up the project."

They reach the platform where the railroad begins. There really are tracks, caked with rust, starting at a buffer block, from which a clothesline hung with wet washing is tied to the next tree. And there stands the *sad locomotive*. It is a big model from the turn of the century, with a huge boiler and big steel wheels, but everything is covered with rust; the engineer's cab has lost almost all its housing, and only part of the rusty roof struts jut into the sky. Grass has taken root on the steps, and beneath them some bushes are growing, though they apparently have been trimmed now and then. The rusted tracks run straight ahead, and after about five hundred feet they plunge into the dense labyrinth of the jungle. They probably end a few yards farther on, for no cleared right of way can be seen.

Near the tracks are the sad headquarters of the stationmaster. Above the front door we read *Amazon Terminal* in large, splendid letters, but in fact it is nothing more than a slightly sturdier wooden hut on poles. Neglected dogs doze on the narrow veranda, butterflies flutter drunkenly around the house, from the forest the cicadas cry at night.

"Come in," the stationmaster says to Fitzcarraldo, but he declines. He has something painful to say, and he keeps putting it off, not knowing how to get it out. He pulls himself together and clears his throat.

"The rails, you see. The thing is, we've come here because of another project, a very big one. Our whole financial situation will change overnight, if it works. What I'm trying to say is, we need the rails."

The stationmaster is dumbfounded, and his face turns gray and old. Night is falling.


## Jungle Railroad, Early Morning

It is getting light. Fitzcarraldo's crew is busy prying the rails off the wooden ties with crowbars. Everyone is working, lending a hand, except for Huerequeque, who is chasing one of his maids into the darkness of the forest. Jaime de Aguila looks up quickly; something like that does not escape his attention. The zebu cow is grazing between the tracks.

The stationmaster is in a state of shock, his eyes gazing into the void; he rushes around from one to the other, having to look on helplessly as his railroad is dismantled bit by bit. As a small group of men start to loosen the big spikes near the locomotive, he comes back to life, a desperate resistance surging up from within. "No, not these, please not these." He hurries over to Fitzcarraldo, who is working in the midst of a group of men and obviously wishes he could hide himself among them.

"Don Fitzcarraldo," the stationmaster gasps, "the men are taking away the rails by the locomotive as well. I beg you, leave at least a few yards around the locomotive, or how can I keep it in shape? Thirty yards would be enough for me, just to roll it back and forth."

Fitzcarraldo looks up. He has to answer for this.

"Stop your men, for God's sake. Look there, in the jungle, the entire route continues on two tracks," says the stationmaster.

"Hey," Fitzcarraldo calls to his men, "we don't need those, there are some more out in the forest."

From the bottom of his broken heart, the stationmaster looks gratefully at Fitzcarraldo.

## On Board, Bridge

The boat is again sailing up the main river. Jaime, the captain, stands outside at the railing with a cord to which a tin cup is attached. Fitzcarraldo, in the wheelhouse, is poring intently over a map.

"We must have passed the Pachitea a long way back," he says.

"No, we haven't," says Jaime.

"But according to the map . . ." Fitzcarraldo ventures hesitantly.

"Then the map must be wrong," says Jaime.

"How can you be so sure?" asks Fitzcarraldo.

Jaime lowers the cup down into the water and then pulls it back up by the string. He carefully tastes the brownish water, like a chef sampling a sauce. "No river tastes like the Pachitea. It's just ahead of us."

## Amazon River, Mouth of the Pachitea

The boat pushes on in its normal course; the river stretches out into the distance. The smokestack puffs evenly, and the engines work in their gentle rhythm. Toward the left riverbank, a little ahead, we see the mouth of the Pachitea. At first glance it is not recognizable as a separate river, since the main branch of the Amazon divides up again and again into individual branches with islands interspersed, so that the confluence of two or more branches always looks like the confluence of entire tributary systems. At this point, however, much darker, almost brownish-black water comes flowing in distinctly in a straight line, set off from the rest as clearly as a knife slice. The horizon is wide, always with more sky than land, and in the sky mountains of clouds are towering high, whole countries, whole continents swelling up, joining and flowing into one another.

## On Board, Bridge

Jaime de Aguila is steering the boat, keeping a sharp eye out for shallows and driftwood. In some places we see extensive flat sandbars, and it doesn't seem easy to find the navigable waters, even though the river is easily a kilometer across. In the cramped wheelhouse are a compass and other nautical instruments, beautifully set in brass. Fitzcarraldo stands beside Jaime, staring at the river ahead and at a detailed map in front of him. Jaime casts him a furtive glance, and they nod to each other. Jaime throws the rudder to the left, and from now on, the voyage follows a different course.

## On Board, Lower Deck

Part of the crew hangs around the galley door like bluebottle flies, and some are hanging onto the window as well, annoying and horny. A girl's hand playfully slaps a rag at one of the more aggressive ones.

The zebu cow is asleep on the lower deck on a bed of fresh leaves, twitching its ears to get rid of the flies.

Farther up the deck, in an area free of cabins, is a long, heavy, polished wooden table with beautiful fixed mahogany stools. Some men are lolling about there, playing cards and boozing. They are so tanked up that they are playing as if in slow motion. One is asleep, bent forward with his head on the table. Suddenly he wakes up and looks around in surprise; he is the only one who has noticed the change of course.

"*Su madre*," he says, drawing out his words, "where are we going, *puta su madre!*" The card players lower their cards and stare at him.

The men leave the galley door, turn and scrutinize the riverbank before them.

"What?" one of them says. "Hey, what's that?"

"Amigos," says Huerequeque, stretching his body out of the galley, tenderly stroking the rifle in his hand, "this is the Pachitea, well known for its native hospitality. Nobody told you that, did they?"


## On Board, Bridge

Stan leans in the door of the wheelhouse with a worried expression and speaks to Fitzcarraldo in a low voice. "Something's brewing down below," he says. "The crew doesn't quite agree with the course, to put it mildly. I must say, I'd like to know myself where the hell we're going."

"I'm coming," says Fitzcarraldo curtly.

## Lower Deck

The crew has assembled; even the mechanic has appeared, smeared with oil, and only Huerequeque and his two young assistants are missing. Besides Wilbur and Stan there are fourteen other men, standing in a semicircle, angry and belligerent.

"Where is Huerequeque?" asks Fitzcarraldo.

"He said he'd rather relax a bit with the señoritas, he knows where we're going anyway," says a sinister-looking man with an open shirt and tattoos on his arm.

"Okay," Fitzcarraldo says. He takes a deep breath. "What did I say in Iquitos?" he asks them. "I need men, real men, not pansies who shit in their pants, understand? You can go straight back to Iquitos. Who wants to go back to Iquitos?"

Fitzcarraldo seems to know his men well; not one wants to go back to Iquitos. He prods them further. "I'll pay your full wages at once. Whoever wants to return to Iquitos, step forward."

Silence, hostility, but no one steps forward. One of the crew is a man as strong as a bear, his cheek stuffed with chewing tobacco. First he shifts it to one side, spits out the brown juice, and then speaks up. "Where are we going?" he says threateningly. "We want to know," he says, pausing to spit again, "what course we're taking."

"We are going up the Pachitea, about three days' journey," Fitzcarraldo says very calmly, as if it were the most harmless kind of destination.

"But Saramiriza is only one day away," interjects the man with the tattoos, "and then what?"

"You can stay in Saramiriza and become missionaries if you want," says Fitzcarraldo.

"Fitz," Stan joins in, "I'll do everything with you, everything really. We've got rifles with us and rails and tools, and provisions for months. I'll do anything you want, you know I'm not afraid, but I would really like to know what you're up to."

Fitzcarraldo just stands there. After a long pause he starts talking. "You know, my plan is so wild that I'm not quite sure myself if it's going to work. We're going up the Pachitea two days past Saramiriza. We have the precise maps from the expedition of '96. I am planning something *geographical*. If it succeeds, we'll all be richer than in our wildest dreams."

"Do you know," asks the one with the chewing tobacco, "how many started in '96, and how many came back?"

"I know," says Fitzcarraldo, "but this isn't '96 any more. Once we get there, we'll see, and I'll explain everything to you."

The crew is not really satisfied, but no one wants to leave the ship, that is clear. Sullenly the assembly disperses.

# Saramiriza, Missionary Station

An oppressively hot, sultry day: dangerously slow the sky is hatching its thunderstorm, which does not want to form just yet. The river flows so sluggishly that it seems afraid to move. The air is still, the forest motionless, the flies alone are buzzing malevolently. The missionary station lies dormant there, some huts in a square, one of them faintly reminiscent of something like western civilization. Along the front of the square is a small church with a tin roof on which vultures are dozing, contemplating carrion; some are even perched on the faded wooden cross on the gable. In front of the church, fastened to a tree limb, hangs a bell without a clapper. Beside it, strung up on a wire, dangles a piece of iron, just the right size for striking the bell.

The buildings face a flat plaza on which a freshly mown lawn, with stripes of reddish clay, has been planted. The lawn is divided geometrically by paths sprinkled with sand. In the middle, where the paths meet, a whitewashed flagpole stands, fenced by a pathetic wrought-iron railing. By the flagpole the pupils stand in quasi-military formation, divided into groups like teams of gymnasts. They all wear khaki shorts and have their hair shorn, yet their Indian features create a strange, incongruous contrast to their formation. Far from them, on the bank of the Pachitea, stand two Jesuit padres in clean, light-colored cassocks; one of them is already rather old and has a white, biblical beard. Both look like men who have worked long, hard years in the jungle. Where they are standing on the riverbank, the river has torn holes many feet deep. Large, loose clumps of earth still hang down over the river, and there are deep fissures in the lawn. Soon part of the empty square will have disappeared. One of the buildings on the riverbank is abandoned, half collapsed, teetering on the edge of the scarp. Pilings have been driven into the bank to prevent its deterioration, but the law of the river has visibly gained the upper hand.

All is motionless, expectant. Then, suddenly, a boy standing alone by the bell starts beating the clapper against it. The result is a rather miserable, almost tinny sound. In the middle of the square the flag is being hoisted, a heavy, limp fabric which refuses to unfurl in the stationary sultriness of the air. At the moment Fitzcarraldo's ship comes into view of the square, the children begin to sing the Peruvian national anthem, in Spanish and horribly out of tune.

The ship docks and the gangplank is lowered, which is no simple task since part of the bank crumbles away immediately. Fitzcarraldo is the first to step ashore. He greets the two missionaries with a handshake.

"Welcome to Saramiriza," the elder one says. "We thought you were a government commission; no one else ever comes here."

"We would like to spend the night here," says Fitzcarraldo. "Could we bring our cow ashore? You really have nice grass here."

"Yes, of course," says the younger one. "You may do that, but you must tether her farther away from the riverbank, or else she'll loosen the soil here with her hooves, as you can see for yourself. We have been forced to give up three buildings already, and if this keeps up we'll have to abandon the station soon. Terrible. The Lord is incomprehensible in his resolutions. For twenty years we've been building this mission, and now this."

"I'd like very much to talk with you," says Fitzcarraldo.


## Missionary Building, Night

Night encloses the main building of the mission. A simple table has been set for the guests with white linen, upon which stand several glasses of fresh mango juice. Braided cane chairs surround the table outside on the plain veranda; around it sit the two missionaries, Fitzcarraldo, and Jaime de Aguila. In the background, illuminated by a kerosene lamp, we see the interior of the building. There are almost no solid walls. There are two beds covered with light-colored mosquito nets, simple chairs, and an extremely austere table. Outside on the convocation square, not far from the boat, the crew has kindled a big fire. There is drinking and noise. Occasionally Huerequeque's señoritas can be heard laughing and shrieking, but Fitzcarraldo pretends not to hear it, feeling embarrassed in front of the two padres. He feigns particular interest in an old school primer he is leafing through.

"Tell me," says Fitzcarraldo, "when I look at this, these texts and pictures, I ask myself how anyone can learn patriotism from a schoolbook?"

"We have a hard time with it," says the younger padre, "but the government requires it; otherwise we wouldn't be allowed to stay on here. You'd never believe how difficult the simplest things are out here: I could tell you about our vaccination program for hours."

"People just refuse to be inoculated," the elder padre says. "But the children, that's easier, they all feel like little Peruvians already. The other day I asked them in class: What is an Indian? Are you Indians? And they said no, we are not Indians; the others farther upstream, they are Indians, not us. And when I asked, what are Indians, they told me: Indians are people who can't read, and who don't know how to wash their clothes."

"And the older people?" asks Jaime in the ensuing pause.

"Well," says the elder missionary, first taking a hesitant sip from his glass, "we can't seem to cure them of their basic notion that our normal life is just an illusion, behind which lies the reality of dreams. In a certain way this does relate to our basic concept of Salvation, but. . . ."

"This interests me very much," interrupts Fitzcarraldo, suddenly attentive. "You see, I am a man of the opera."

## Mission, Convocation Square

The men are flocked around a big campfire, drinking,
singing songs, and yelling. Standing around them, still
and solemn, are Jívaros from the station, their dark eyes
gleaming in the semi-darkness. Huerequeque's señoritas
are the center of attention, they are being passed about
and fondled. The girls laugh and rap the knuckles of the
impertinent men. Suddenly a fight erupts in the dimness,
two men become entangled in a scuffle.

## Missionary Station

The padres and their two guests are still sitting around
the table as before. Jaime de Aguila now leads the
conversation.

"What do you know," he asks, "about the Jívaros on
the upper course? I was there during the disaster in '96;
have you had any contact since then?"

"Yes, eight years ago, not so long after your misfortune," says the younger missionary, "two of our brothers
set off with some natives. One of them returned a day
later and said that the Jívaros had withdrawn deep into the
forest. After that we heard nothing for weeks. And then,
as you probably heard, one of our brothers was washed
up, he was rotting away already. His head was gone, and
they had filled his belly with stones. But it was God's will

that this outrage should come to light, and He let the corpse appear when the water had dropped."

"Ah, that was the time when the military planned a retaliatory expedition," says Jaime.

"But nothing came of it," says the elderly missionary. "There was a lot of talk, but nobody did anything. Since then we've had no contact. Now and then a canoe shows up, the people are peaceful enough and want to trade, but really we don't know anything. Anyway, what do you want up there?"

"We are planning something geographical," says Fitzcarraldo. This has apparently became his standard reply.

From outside the noise is getting wild, it can no longer be ignored or hushed up. Jaime rises. "Padres, please excuse me for a moment, I must attend to things outside. The men . . ."

We see that Jaime de Aguila is assuming an increasingly dominant role. In the darkness we hear him shouting at the men, and quiet is restored almost immediately. In the ensuing lull, only the mosquitoes can be heard, buzzing malevolently. Fitzcarraldo is slapping at them.

"You have to get used to them, young man," says the elder missionary to Fitzcarraldo, who isn't so young himself. "We have more than enough of them."

The first faraway, soundless flashes of lightning pierce the distant sky. "I hope the rain comes soon," says Fitzcarraldo.

## Saramiriza, Missionary Station, Next Day

Dawn is breaking, misty stripes hover over the dark river, and the jungle is steaming. The birds greet the day with their infernal jubilation. It has rained during the night. The grass on the convocation square is glistening wet, and puddles have formed in the red clay. All men are on board. Children stand mutely on the riverbank, looking at the ship. The two padres are with them. On board, on the lower deck, there is noise and confusion. We can't quite make out what it's about from this distance, but most likely the battle for the señoritas has flared up again. One of them is bickering angrily. The men are pushing and shoving each other.

## On Board, Bridge

Jaime de Aguila has taken Fitzcarraldo aside. Serious and resolute, he demonstratively removes his captain's cap, which he hasn't worn in a long time and obviously has put on only to enhance his gesture.

"You must crack down on the men now, and I mean at once," he says, "or else I quit, and you can find yourself a new captain!"

"Who is it?" asks Fitzcarraldo.

"It's Evaristo Chávez and Fabiano, the Brazilian. They're the main ones, and then the señoritas, they must be put ashore immediately. I mean immediately, or you can steer this tub yourself. And Huerequeque, I don't trust him an inch either."

"But he's cunning," says Fitzcarraldo. "He may booze a lot, but he's got more brains than the rest of them put together."

"The rest," Jaime says disdainfully, "they aren't worth much, either. Go on, do something, you're the boss."

## On Board, Lower Deck

Fitzcarraldo descends the bronze-trimmed stairway from the bridge, and at once the quarreling dies down. Unruffled, he plants himself serenely behind the mess table and counts out four piles of money, one beside the other; casually, almost offhand, he calls, "Evaristo! Fabiano! And the two señoritas!"

The four step forward with foreboding.

"Your services," says Fitzcarraldo, "are no longer required. I thank you. Here is your wage till the end of the week. You have two minutes to get your things. To put it more precisely, in a hundred and twenty seconds you're off the ship."

This hits home. Huerequeque, who has just taken a step forward to say something, stands rooted to the spot and doesn't make a sound. The four of them leave the ship, and one of the señoritas is crying.

"Maybe we are the lucky ones," says Fabiano somberly as he leaves the ship.

## Pachitea, Early in the Day

The *Molly Aida* follows its course up the middle of the river. To the left and right the jungle towers above the waters, but for this it pays a big price. Here and there, trees on the riverbank have been uprooted and have crashed into the watery clay; in some places the bank has been so undermined that entire groves of trees are searching in the void with their bunched roots, while in other places big clumps of earth have been washed away along with several trees. Branches stick up out of the water, swaying and shaking their denial against the current. Fog still hovers in the treetops, which obliviously grow, crowd each other out, give birth, and are overgrown with lianas, engulfed, rotting. The trees sweat and sleep and doze and grow and fight for the light and lie dormant and in the morning, after a night of rain, they piss, like cows, hundreds of thousands of them, a hundred thousand million. And that makes the birds happy, and they screech, ten times a hundred thousand million.

Tense expectation settles ponderously over the decks. No one is sleeping or drinking or playing cards. All the men are leaning side by side over the railing, staring silently into the dusky green of the forest. Up ahead the first hills emerge, overgrown by the jungle, with clouds of fog billowing up the slopes. The forest falls strangely silent, as if it wanted to hold its breath.

Time passes, slowly. On the bridge Fitzcarraldo searches the forest with his binoculars. Nothing.

Then suddenly, from a distance, from the depths of the forest, comes the sound of drums, at first almost inaudible, wafting away with the fog. Then they get stronger, closer. Huerequeque steals quietly to his galley and cautiously grabs his rifle. One after another the men follow his example. Only Wilbur seems to feel fine, lounging in his barber chair, soon to become his throne.

On the bridge, Jaime de Aguila bends down to the speaking tube that connects him with the engine room. "Choke the engine, half speed ahead," he says.

"Half speed ahead," the funnel replies.

"What are the men doing?" asks Jaime.

Fitzcarraldo leans over the railing and looks down to the lower decks. "They've armed themselves," he says.

"On no account are they to shoot," says Jaime. "If there is any shooting, then we're lost. That's exactly the mistake we made on the first expedition. They are only to shoot if we're directly attacked. Go down and tell them that, or there might be another disaster."


## Jungle by the Pachitea, Night

With our eyes we scan the edge of the forest; our glance moves very slowly, seeking to penetrate the depths of the shadowy forest. But nothing stirs; there is only the dim silence and the hollow, rumbling, incessant drumming of a whole group of drums at once. The sound is disquieting, menacing, coming closer, swelling up. Our eyes burn with the strain, yet we can see *absolutely nothing*.

## *Aboard Ship*

Fitzcarraldo climbs atop the uppermost roof with his phonograph, to the small wooden platform. Now it's Caruso's turn, he says to himself. "The cow," he calls down, "put the cow right up at the bow, right in front so she can be seen."

This is done. Huerequeque is the driving force. "I bet those bare-asses have never seen anything like this," he says. "That'll teach 'em respect." There is a sudden, hard thud beside Huerequeque's head, and an arrow as long as his arm vibrates in the cabin wall with an evil twang.

"All right," says Huerequeque, "this is it."

The men spring into motion; most of them dive for cover, and one of them jerks up his rifle.

"Don't shoot, you asshole!" roars Jaime from the bridge overhead. The man lowers his rifle and flees into one of the open cabins.

And then, suddenly, Fitzcarraldo's music resounds, the voice of Caruso, sad and beautiful and stately and very scratchy. The music mixes with the drums, swells up against them, and gradually silences them. One drum after the other falls silent.

Wilbur jumps up and dances a strange, ecstatic dance on deck. He is the only one visible. From the forest, silence comes back. Only the ship vibrates gently, the engine chugs softly, the forward movement is barely perceptible, almost at a standstill. "My armies," says Wilbur, "have reported for duty."

Up on the bridge, Fitzcarraldo has spotted something with his binoculars. "There's a canoe," he says, "I can just see the rear part, it must have been drawn ashore fast." Through the binoculars, we can see that he is right. Between the hanging branches of a big tree, whose twigs reach down into the water, lies an Indian dugout, half hidden and partially drawn ashore. Besides this, nothing. The jungle seems to be paralyzed with emotion by Caruso's beautiful, sad voice.

## On the Bridge

The music is over. A foreboding silence pervades the jungle, nothing moves, even the birds are mute. Jaime strains to listen, and Fitzcarraldo stares ahead intently.

"There are silences and silences," says Jaime. "And I don't like this one."

Fitzcarraldo has discovered something. "I can see something. There's something on the water."

Jaime can't see it.

"Something black," says Fitzcarraldo, "on the water, floating toward us."

## Water of the Río Pachitea

Something black drifts on the water of the Pachitea. It comes closer, it's not large. Like a black bowl with a small mast. Then we see what it is: a black umbrella, opened up and placed on the water like a nutshell, the handle sticking up in the air like a mast — an ominous object of unknown meaning.

## On Board, Lower Deck

Fitzcarraldo leans far over the railing and fishes out the umbrella with a pole. The men, armed, cluster around him.

"What the hell is an umbrella doing here?" asks Fitzcarraldo.

"The Jívaros took it off one of the missionaries they killed," Huerequeque surmises. "The gentlemen in the forest mean it as a last warning. They love flowery gestures."

## Fitzcarraldo's Cabin, Night

Fitzcarraldo has called almost everyone to his cabin, which is simply arranged but a bit larger than the rest. The men crouch all over, packed into the room. Some are smoking, and the fumes fill the air.

"From now on," says Fitzcarraldo, "everything depends on how we behave. With the first expedition, they were expecting the ship. Word had gotten around that some sort of divine vehicle was on its way, with Viracocha, the White God, sent to lead the Jívaros out of the jungle. The Jívaros probably left the interior of Brazil about three hundred years ago, and for ten generations they've been criss-crossing the jungle. It often happened that whole tribes began to wander."

"Yes," agrees Jaime de Aguila, "their language doesn't belong to any of the language groups that settled around here: the Huambisas, the Shapras, the Campas, all belong to a quite different language family."

"These Jívaros," says Fitzcarraldo, "were driven by religious faith to seek a land without sorrow and death, and, at the end of their pilgrimage, a White God, Viracocha, would lead them there. We have to take advantage of this. But this God doesn't come with cannons, he comes with the voice of Caruso."

"What the hell has that got to do with us," says the man with the tattoos. "If a bare-ass gets too close to me he'll get one right between the eyes."

"The good Lord doesn't mean shit to us," says one.

"Let others stick out their ass for the good Lord, not us," another murmurs.

Things don't look too good. The atmosphere reeks of growing mutiny.

"Sometimes I think," another man challenges, "that you're missing a few screws somewhere. This here ain't no stage play. Those boys out there in the woods mean business."

And deep down Fitzcarraldo knows it's true; he feels it too, and he says no more.


## On Deck, Night

Darkness surrounds the boat. It is pitch black. Some of the men, standing watch with their rifles, are straining their eyes, staring out into the night. The forest is filled with millions of wailing, croaking sounds coming from tiny tree frogs. Into the darkness, an entire universe is croaking sad messages. We too strain our ears to listen: wasn't there something, aren't there human voices among them, exchanging wailing messages about a sneak attack?

Fitzcarraldo gently puts his hand on one man's shoulder. "Go and sleep, I'll handle this now," he says in a low voice. "At four o'clock someone else can take over from me."

The man nods and glides over the darkened deck toward the cabins. The engine is chugging softly.

## Fitzcarraldo's Cabin, Next Day

The darkness of night is over, and day slips through the wooden shutters in streaks of light. Fitzcarraldo lies under his mosquito net, sleeping soundly. Wilbur enters, cheerful, almost casual. He lifts the mosquito net and wakes Fitzcarraldo, who bolts upright with a jerk. He instantly grabs his rifle, which he has taken to bed with him.

"Fitz," says Wilbur, very friendly, "we'll be having breakfast alone."


## On Deck

Rifle in hand and hardly dressed, Fitzcarraldo rushes on deck. There he finds only the mechanic, bent over the railing and staring bewildered after something. Fitzcarraldo looks too. We look with him. There, in the middle of the misty waters of the Pachitea, a lifeboat is floating, jammed with the crew. They are rowing like crazy, rapidly vanishing downstream in the morning mist.

"Why didn't you go with them?" asks Fitzcarraldo sarcastically.

"I didn't know anything about it, I was below deck in the engine room the whole time," the man says.

## Bridge

Fitzcarraldo comes rushing up the stairs and tears open the door to the wheelhouse. There Stan is kneeling, bent over Jaime de Aguila lying on the floor, and is loosening the ropes on his arms and legs with nervous movements. Jaime pulls the gag from his mouth in a rage.

"These pigs," he says, "all of a sudden there they all were with their rifles. I said all along they were good for nothing."

"Wilbur's still here, and the mechanic," says Fitzcarraldo. "I thought we were all alone." Outside the drums start to drone again.

"It seems to me," says Fitzcarraldo, that we're now in great need of some Italian opera."

## Pachitea

The ship is now in the midst of the last foothills of the Andes. To the left and right there are small but very steep mountains emerging from the morning fog. The smokestack is fuming, but the boat makes so little headway that it almost seems to be stationary, it pushes along so slowly. The music of grand opera wafts over from the boat to the forest and, as before, the drumming soon stops altogether.

## Bridge

The five men remaining are holding a brief council of war in the crowded wheelhouse. All of them, except Wilbur, carry rifles. Fitzcarraldo is composed and speaks quite calmly. "The dream," he says, "is over. That was it, gentlemen. We'll have to turn back. Stan will stay up here with you, and you go back down to the engine room."

"Sure," the mechanic says, "I will. I can manage."

We look closely at the mechanic for the first time; slender and young and smeared with grease, he had always been inconspicuous to us. But now, in this hour of distress, the young man seems to have class, even if he would rather have taken off as well. He seems to have gained some power now.

"And I'll take over the center deck with Wilbur," Fitzcarraldo says. "We'll make a 180-degree turn. Can we do that here?"

"We can," says Jaime, the captain.

Before each of them heads for his post, Fitzcarraldo again quickly scans the edge of the jungle to the right and left. The Italian opera on the roof reaches a crescendo. Fitzcarraldo leans out the window and looks back. Very slowly, as if in slow motion, he pulls his head in again.

"Won't work," he says, his words drawled, yet laconic.

"What?" asks Stan, not comprehending.

"If you would all please turn around very slowly, but no sudden movements, nice and slow."

Moving as one man, they all turn around slowly and look out the rear window.

"Do you see what I see?" asks Fitzcarraldo.

At last we share the same view. Abruptly we realize that across the entire breadth of the river, the way back is blocked by dugouts, at least forty or more, following a short distance behind, perhaps a ship's length away. Each canoe is manned by three or four Indians, paddling very smoothly and carefully maintaining a precise distance from the creeping steamboat. And now we see, farther back in the fog, more canoes appearing. We can tell from a distance that the Indians have long hair, their faces are painted with ochre stripes, and they seem to carry weapons. But they only follow slowly, at a cautious distance.

"Great," says Fitzcarraldo, "this is just what we needed."

"We have to keep going ahead," Jaime says, gritting his teeth, "whether we want to or not. Breaking through back there would be the end of us." He turns to the mechanic. "You go down to the engine room now, nice and easy, no abrupt movements, understand? We should put on a bit more steam, but very delicately. I think it would be good to pick up a little speed." With calm, controlled movements the mechanic slips out of the wheelhouse.

The Indians continue following at a distance. We see how the propeller at the stern gently starts producing a stronger backwash, the engine adds power and the boat picks up a little speed. Trailing them at the same distance, the Jívaros' canoes also step up the pace. We notice that their numbers have increased in the meantime.

In the wheelhouse, Fitzcarraldo stares through the window toward the rear. He looks through his binoculars. "They're all men, some of them have spears," he says softly. "They're keeping their distance." He turns to Jaime. "Did you experience anything like this in '96?"

"No," says Jaime, "I've never seen anything like this in my entire life."

The music on the roof stops, the cylinder is finished.

"I don't think our friends like this," says Fitzcarraldo. "It seems to make them nervous when *Tosca* is finished."


*Pachitea*

At some distance, seen from the riverbank. The steamboat glides upstream of necessity, now followed by probably a hundred canoes. Small but recognizable, Fitzcarraldo creeps slowly up to his phonograph on the roof. An overture begins, loud and exquisite and scratchy. The boats are trailing in a great procession. The fog has lifted above the treetops. On the center deck, the *patient cow* stands and gazes.

## On Board, Bridge, Toward Evening

Jaime the captain and Fitzcarraldo are standing soaked with sweat and exhausted, staring straight ahead. A prolonged silence. Without seeing the canoes again, we know that they are right on their tail.

"How long can this go on?" asks Fitzcarraldo.

"Until we run onto a sandbank," says Jaime curtly. "But I think it's best to keep moving. If we do anything now it could be the worst move possible, for one reason or another. The initiative has to come from them."


## On Board, Quarterdeck

At the stern of the ship. We realize to our horror that Wilbur, completely unprotected, is gesticulating wildly in the direction of the Jívaros in the canoes beyond. He performs a strange courtship dance and mouths great soundless cries in a language familiar only to those on the far shore of madness. He lures the canoes with the seductive movements of his wooing body. He summons his whole army. And indeed, three or four of the canoes in front come closer, hesitantly. One is extremely close now, almost at arm's length. Altogether there must be four hundred canoes now following the *Molly Aida*.

## Bridge

In alarm, Jaime suddenly sees what is happening with Wilbur. "Wilbur," he shouts, and with an obviously mistaken reflex, he pulls the lever to sound the foghorn.

## Quarterdeck

Precisely at the moment when the foremost Jívaro touches the hull with his fingertips, the foghorn issues its mighty blast. The Indian pulls back his hand at once as if he got an electrical shock from the contact. As when a gust of wind swirls into a pile of leaves and scatters them, the canoes whirl away in horror from the boat. Slowly they regroup again into a formation, like a school of tiny fish after they have been scattered.

## Bridge

Jaime breathes a sigh of relief. "Excuse me," he says. "I almost ruined it."

The sudden event has loosened Fitzcarraldo up, making him almost cheerful. He leans his rifle beside the wheel and goes to the door, perfectly normal, as if he were somewhere in the harbor of Iquitos. "I think I'll take over now," he says, "the sun is going down soon."

## On Board

Fitzcarraldo comes down the steps, quite relaxed, crosses the deck past the astonished Stan, who lies under cover between two rolls of cable with his rifle aimed.

"Hope that thing doesn't go off by itself," Fitzcarraldo kids him, stepping up to Wilbur. "Well, Wilbur, now we'll wave our friends to come on over," he says. With the senseless courage of fools and visionaries, he stands and waves.

And then, suddenly, another one of their kind joins them. One of the cabin doors opens and Huerequeque appears, blinking sleepily, just waking up from his binge. He is barefoot and wearing only his pants, and his naked belly bulges down over his belt.

"Hola, brethren," he says to the natives, "what time is it anyway? Amigos!" he shouts. "Come on, you bare-ass sons of bitches — there's beer for everyone!"

Fitzcarraldo is momentarily rigid with amazement; he stares at him as if he were seeing a ghost. "Where did you come from, Huerequeque?" he asks. "This can't be true."

"I just had a nap," says Huerequeque. "Did the others take off already, those cowards, those *degeneraditos*?"

During this moment of utter innocence and ease, the biggest canoe has tied up to the side of the ship, unnoticed, and a dignified man, with a particularly beautiful feather headdress braided into his hair, apparently one of the chiefs, has boarded with two companions. They are unarmed except for fishing spears with long shafts. Fitzcarraldo is the first to see them.

"Keep quiet," he says, "I don't think they'll harm us."
Fitzcarraldo extends a hand to the chief, intending to
grasp his, but the Indian merely brushes over Fitzcarraldo's fingertips with his own fingertips, very lightly, a
soft, tender, beautiful first touch. Wilbur and Huerequeque get the same careful, shy touch.

The chief begins to speak, very calmly and dignified; in
the meantime he and his companions now and then spit
casually through their teeth onto the floor.

"We need Jaime," says Fitzcarraldo.

## Pachitea

Evening has descended over the river, and there the boat
is lying now, still under steam but moored to several
strong trees on the riverbank. It is surrounded by a thick
swarm of canoes, all pressing close, hands hoping to touch
the hull of the ship. At first glance it looks as if all the
danger and apprehension is over for the moment. Between the trees, the first campfires are being kindled; the
Indians seem to be making preparations for the night.

## On Board, Evening

An enchanting spectacle, the sky is consumed by red-orange flames. The last screeching flocks of parrots seek their sleeping trees for the night. The wailing tree frogs begin their nightly orgies of grief for the state of the universe. The million-fold croaking sets in.

On the center deck sits the whole remaining crew, huddled together, and, in a wide semicircle around them, about seventy Indians. They have brought some clay on deck, confined within a square of thick wooden clubs, upon which burns one of their typical fires: three tree trunks arranged to form a star, with some thinner dry branches in the gaps to feed the flames, and on top, placed directly on the glowing trunks, a broad earthenware pot, in which something is simmering. One or two Indians take turns talking, and for the first time we have time enough to listen to their peculiar soft-sounding language. There seems to be a hierarchy dictating who is to say what and when. The gestures of their hands are striking and beautiful, foreign, gentle — they move their hands like conductors scanning an inaudible, unknown melody that falters into the light from the darkest, most mysterious depths of the forest. It is a cautiousness, a shyness beyond compare.

A silent lull ensues. Jaime begins to translate.

"They're talking about the white vessel, meaning our ship," he says. "I think they expect something like salvation from it. They say a curse is weighing on the entire landscape here. They know that we are no gods, but the ship seems to be making a big impression on them, and they keep talking about the voice on the roof. I think they want us to stay with them, and the chief says he wants to give us a present."

Wilbur beams with enthusiasm. "The Jívaros," he says, "my people! I have found my people. We shall establish a kingdom with them."

The chief rises and hands Fitzcarraldo two live turtles that have been pierced in front on the projecting rim of their shells and bound to each other with a liana string. Then he fills a bowl with the dark liquid boiling on the fire.

"Drink," Jaime says between his teeth. "It is *chushuási,* a little bitter, but it won't kill you."

Fitzcarraldo drinks bravely, as he is told. He lowers the bowl and passes it on to his men, obeying a gesture from the chief. "Friends," he says in a low voice, almost to himself, "I think this voyage continues."

Night has fallen darkly, the faint glimmer of the fire is reflected seventy-fold in the dark eyes of the Jívaros.

## On Board

The new day fades in, bearing rain which cascades down steadily, indifferently. The whole center deck is filled with Indians; about a hundred of them are huddled silently on board, looking straight ahead. The boat steams slowly and smoothly up the river, while behind and around it throng the Indian canoes, now very close. The jungle slopes are not very high, but steep, and behind them we see towering cloud-veiled slopes, the first hint of the eastern edge of the Andes. Right in the midst of the natives, Wilbur moves about, completely at ease. Stan, who is with him, seems to be a bit more mistrustful.

## Bridge

Fitzcarraldo is poring over detailed maps, and beside him Jaime is steering. Huerequeque has moved over to him and stares over Fitzcarraldo's shoulder. Fitzcarraldo straightens up to his full height. "There, up ahead," he says to Jaime, "yes there, do you see that range of hills?"

"I see it," says Jaime. "That must be it."

"We're here," says Fitzcarraldo and turns to Huerequeque: "This slope may look insignificant, but it's going to be my *destiny*."

Huerequeque has a knowing look on his face.

## Heights of Camisea

The boat has anchored; there is nothing to indicate why *here,* of all places, nothing distinguishes this spot. Like everywhere else, the jungle simply grows up the slope, damp and steaming. It is still raining. Farther ahead a more conspicuous mountain rises up steeply from the river.

Fitzcarraldo has gone ashore with his companions, and almost every Indian on deck has followed them. Fitzcarraldo is trying to keep his maps dry by hiding them under his shirt. A footpath, bearing the distinct imprints of many naked feet, starts here and snakes up the hill.

"Follow me," says Fitzcarraldo.

"Now he's showing his cards," says Huerequeque.


## Atop the Ridge

Fitzcarraldo has counted the steps. He is peering around in the jungle. Vaguely we realize with him that the summit of the slope must have been reached. Fitzcarraldo pauses solemnly and waits until his crew and the Indians on the path have caught up to him.

"This is it. This is what we were looking for, right here."

Stan and the mechanic look around in amazement; there is nothing here, just ordinary, dense jungle, like everywhere else.

"We'll have to climb a tree for you dimwits to figure it out," says Huerequeque. With his machete he hacks his way through a tangle of roots and lianas to a giant tree. "We shall build a viewing platform for these gentlemen."

## Treetop, Heights of Camisea

In the expansive crown of a giant tree a narrow, temporary platform has been built, adroitly lashed tight with
lianas. Fitzcarraldo and his friends are crowded together
up there. There isn't room for all of them, so Stan and the
mechanic have to perch lower down in a forked branch,
but from there they can still see enough.

"I don't believe it," says Stan.

Now we see what they see, as we follow Fitzcarraldo's
pointing hand. The dark, clay-brown upper course of the
Pachitea stretches below us, and when we turn our gaze to
the other side, where the slope descends again, we suddenly see, so close we can almost touch it, a much
broader, much lighter river. At this point it reaches close
to us in a bellying curve, but then turns away again to lose
itself in another direction between the mountains.

"That's the Ucayali," says Fitzcarraldo. "And all the
upper course belongs to us."

"I knew it!" says Huerequeque. "We're going to build
a railway tunnel."

"No," says Fitzcarraldo, "we'll drag the ship over the
mountain — and the bare-asses are going to help us!"

"How the hell are we going to do that?" asks Jaime.

"Just like the cow jumped over the moon."

Emotion overwhelms the men in the treetop: so this is
the goal, this is the task. A grandiose music, full of pathos,
sets in as we look from the Ucayali to the Pachitea, and
from the Pachitea to the Ucayali, and back again, amid
the screams of the chattering monkeys. It is uplifting, we

begin to soar, drunk with joy we rise with the wafting music high above the land. There they are, the two rivers, converging toward each other at a single point, and between them the heights of Camisea, densely overgrown with jungle, the mountan that is Fitzcarraldo's fate. Here it is, *his challenge,* the challenge of the impossible.

## *Jungle, Heights of Camisea*

It rains. It rains solidly. It rains in heavy, dense streams. A giant tree, almost fully overgrown with lianas, aged by the pull of wild creepers and the fight for the roof of light, gone old and gray and mossy, suddenly shudders down to its roots. It groans a terrible, almost human groan, then, ever so slowly, it bends forward, bends farther, picks up speed, yes, we scream inside, *it's falling,* the tree *is falling*! It falls in one last bow before human force, before human axes. With a terrible crash the giant collapses to the earth. And there, right next to it, the next one bends, and then another and another; a whole forest is swaying and collapsing.

Deep inside the forest, the foul, moldering slope rises steeply in front of us. There the Indians have lined up along a broad front, hacking away with machetes at the dense jungle growth and knotted liana thickets. Clouds of mosquitoes swarm around them, and from above a drizzling mist of tropical rain is falling. With light, almost dangling movements, the Jívaros wield the razor-sharp machetes with such elegance, such finality in their actions. And still we know that the jungle will close up again on its own, within weeks. As soon as they are cut, the dangling lianas hesitate for a long moment, as if denying at first their own destruction, as if needing a moment to understand, then they crash to the ground, collapsing into themselves. Fleshy bushes are hacked through with a single stroke, their big leaves bending aside as an angry, whitish juice oozes from the cut. Conjuring poison, orchids in heat glare at their reapers.

On two giant trees standing side by side, the Indians have erected head-high scaffolding, making a notch with their axes at the point where the high-ribbed roots unite from all sides in the tree trunk. From the forest the axes resound, and the machetes accompany them with their music, each whistling and ringing in a different tone, depending on what it strikes. Almost casually, an Indian kills a snake with a stick.

A clearing. Several big, flat stones have been placed on the clay ground, and a whole group of Jívaros are waiting their turn to sharpen their machetes. Much like scythes when cutting grass, the machetes must be sharpened after being used a short time. The Jívaros dip the blades briefly into a clay puddle to moisten them, then they hone the blades, pressing them on the stone and, in doing so, bending the steel.

Fitzcarraldo is in the middle of the forest among the toiling Indians, indicating the direction that the towpath must take. We can already see that the jungle has been cleared in a strip about twenty meters wide. The trees crash, and the rain crashes too.


## On Deck, Camisea Landing, Evening

Fitzcarraldo's crew sits around the mess table on the center deck, eating. From an Indian basket lined with fresh leaves, Huerequeque takes a piece of smoked, dark meat, and cuts off a piece for himself.

"Not bad, this wild boar," he says and takes a swig of *aguardiente* from a bulbous basket bottle.

The mood is more contemplative. Jaime de Aguila steps out from the shadows to the table, elaborately kicking the clay off his shoes. Only Wilbur sits apart from the others, by the railing, where he has stretched a linen sheet tautly with some cord. He holds a lamp up very close to it so that the cloth glows white on the other side. Gnats dance toward the luminous spot and huge moths flutter about excitedly; a few have already settled on the glowing material. We see them closer. Some of the moths are strange, almost primeval-looking creatures, as if they have emerged from some deeply buried, distant epoch. Wilbur's breath comes in short excited gasps. Branches from a large tree hang over the deck. The zebu cow sighs aloud in its dream. On land, fires flicker and low voices waft over. The parrot speaks a couple of unintelligible words.

An eleven-year-old Jívaro boy is standing quite naturally by the mess table, now and then joining the circle of conversation with ease, in his own language. Wilbur evidently brought him aboard.

"That was quite a good start," says Fitzcarraldo contentedly. "What do you think, Jaime, will the Indians stick with us?"

Jaime, wrapped in thought, keeps cleaning the soles of his shoes with a piece of wood. "I'm not sure what the Jívaros are really thinking. I spoke with some of them just now, but what's really going on in their minds is a mystery to me. And it'll take us a long time, too. I ask myself if this is going to work out at all."

"If it doesn't," says Huerequeque, "we'll just build a tunnel." But nobody seizes on this idea, and he is alone with it.

"Once the stretch of forest has been cleared, we should be able to manage," says Fitzcarraldo. "Theoretically, I could tow the boat over with one hand tied behind my back, provided I had a perfect pulley system. I would pull a chain as far as two miles, in order to move the ship two inches."

"But that's just theory," says Jaime. "It will take a long time, and we haven't got that much."

"The shipbuilding has cost us two months already," says Fitzcarraldo. "That leaves seven before the option runs out."

The Jívaro boy starts talking. "Our little amigo is absolutely right," says Huerequeque, who of course doesn't understand a thing. "What's his name, anyway? Hey, Wilbur, what's your friend's name?"

"McNamara," says Wilbur. "McNamara is my footman," he says.

"An *aguardiente* for our little footman!" cries Huerequeque, moving to hand the bottle to the boy.

"Leave it," says Fitzcarraldo angrily, "that stuff has ruined enough Indians already."

There is a long silence. Then Jaime brushes a black, almost fist-sized spider off the table with his muddy stick, after it had been sitting there motionless the whole time, attracting more and more attention from the circle of men.


## On Board, Center Deck

The day has begun with light rain, jungle and sky are dripping. A long row of Indians has formed on board, filing past Fitzcarraldo. The Jívaros are half-naked, and some of them carry machetes, spears, and blowpipes, the latter wrapped along the stem with liana strings. Jaime de Aguila is giving each a spoonful of the blackish, sticky goo as they wait. The Indians scrutinize the arrow poison, sniff it, and stuff it into small wooden cases. By Fitzcarraldo stand a few dignitaries, among them the chief who made the first contact.

Stan and the mechanic work strenuously in the background at Fitzcarraldo's ice machine. "I need someone to take over, my arms are falling off," says the mechanic.

"Wilbur," says Fitzcarraldo, "can't you help?"

But Wilbur can't, for he evidently has rubbed his arms with sugarcane brandy the night before, and now he is carrying on his carefully outstretched arms about twenty big, iridescent blue butterflies, that he cannot bear to shoo away.

"We can't count on Huerequeque today, either," says Fitzcarraldo. "he took the *aguardiente* with him to bed."

Beyond we see the whole hillside teeming with Jívaros. Trees are still being cut, and work is proceeding on clearing the towpath. About a hundred men are needed to drag one fallen tree out of the way with liana ropes, levers, and axes. The activity is tremendous. Fleets of canoes are moored at the riverbank with tough cords of liana bark, and for the first time we also see women, most of them carrying children on their backs. They are dressed in tunic-like reddish-brown cloth, their long hair falling down to their shoulders.

Fitzcarraldo lets a shy, hesitant Indian try a test shot with his blowpipe, or else, he says, they might think we're trying to pass honey off on them. The Indian takes a thornlike dart about four inches long from his leather quiver, wraps it in a wad of cotton that he takes from a second quiver, dips the tip into his bowl of sticky poison, and shoves the finished dart into his pipe. Fitzcarraldo steps a little to one side and points to a chicken a few yards forward at the bow, tied with a string on one leg. The

Jívaro fires the dart with a short, strangely hollow-sounding puff of breath and strikes the hen in the side. It spreads its wings with a sudden jerk and goes rigid in the instant paralysis of death. Foam gathers on its beak, forming bubbles. Then the hen topples over, as if frozen, and moves no more. There are murmurs of admiration: the curare is good.

"I just hope it doesn't occur to them to use it on us," says Stan. "The ice is ready!"

Fitzcarraldo goes over to his machine and takes the whitish, gleaming block of ice, partially wrapped in a cloth, from Stan. "Should I really give it to the chief as a present, Jaime?" asks Fitzcarraldo. "You must explain to him that it melts, that there'll be nothing left of it."

"There is no word for ice in their language," says Jaime.

After some hesitation, Fitzcarraldo finally thrusts the block of ice into the arms of the chief. Caught by surprise, he stands as still as a statue, and Fitzcarraldo looks somewhat embarrassed. Some of the Indians fondle the dripping block, deep astonishment in their faces. As in an old photograph they freeze into a tableau as whispers pass down the line. Then we notice the Jívaros up front, who are working to clear the path through the forest. They stop and look over at the boat. Like a brush fire the astonishment spreads up the entire hillside, and we can see how it heads along the slope. In an instant the entire slope is still. Only the river flows, as always, and the rain rains.

## Heights of Camisea

At least two weeks must have passed, for now, as if sliced clean by a taut cord, a cleared strip stretches up through the forest like a ribbon of clay and disappears down the other side. The day is fairly clear; we can now make out the higher mountain ranges in the distance. The cleared stretch gives the impression of a foreign body in the sea, floating in the hilly waves of the jungle. We also see that the terrain is not flat: there are folds in it, and the incline levels off at first before starting up even more steeply. There is even a small gully that has been furrowed in the ground by a brook. Along the towpath the Jívaros have built temporary huts, from which thin smoke pervades the entire jungle in the vicinity.

The steamboat is set diagonally to the Pachitea, tied to the other riverbank with strong, tightly anchored ropes so it cannot drift away. The bow touches the riverbank at its slope, which goes up at a treacherous angle there. From heavy logs an inclined ramp has been built from the water to the slope, in order to lift the bow out of the river. It looks a bit like a heavy, massive bridge, inclined and supported by sturdy pillars. About forty ropes and steel cables are stretched uphill from the bow. An equal number of winches, anchored deeply in the ground with poles and braced by the sawed-off stumps of the strongest giant trees, are scattered along the slope. Each winch has cable wheels with heavy, bulky gearboxes, upon which two beams are set in the form of a huge cross. The beams are chest-high, so that about twenty Indians pushing them in a circle can set them in motion.

The first big moment has arrived. Fitzcarraldo's crew has assembled on deck at the bow and on land by the ramp. Anything not nailed down has been removed from the boat and is spread about on the ground: the lifeboats, all the luggage, parts of the rudder mechanism, cables, rails that haven't been used yet, lie in wild disarray, everything damp and smeared with clay.

All eyes are turned to Fitzcarraldo, who gives the signal to start working. The Jívaros begin pushing in circles on all the winches simultaneously; they turn the crossbeams and a mechanical clicking of ratchets and creaking cogwheels begins. Across the river, the mechanic and some other men prepare to loosen the counter-tension of the ropes. As if in slow motion the steel cables slowly tighten until they are stretched horizontal in the air. With a slight lurch the boat gets stuck on the wood of the ramp, and the bow starts slowly digging into the wood. Somehow things don't look too good; the force of the towing mechanism seems to be set incorrectly. From the terrible pull of the ropes the whole ship groans as the the hull begins to buckle; we can see this from the uppermost supports of the deck housings, which bend slightly to one side. The highest platform on deck contorts, and with a vile noise a plank springs up from the deck and soars into the air. The bow has eaten its way into the slope by the ramp.

"Stop!" roars Huerequeque, "the hull is breaking apart!" Jaime de Aguila shouts something in Jívaro and hurries up the slope because a few of the winch crews are still turning. Everything stops, and an ominous calm spreads.

"Back up!" shouts Huerequeque. "Reverse the tension!" Slowly the tension is released. It takes a long time, since this procedure apparently has not been practiced.

Fitzcarraldo examines the bow with his men. A rivet as thick as a man's thumb has shot free, others are loose. "That almost did it," says Fitzcarraldo.

"I told you," says the mechanic, "we have to divide the boat into at least three or four parts and get them over one by one."

"We rejected that idea a long time ago," Fitzcarraldo says angrily. "We could take it apart easily enough, but to put it back together again we'd need a real shipyard, and where are we going to get one?"

"Compadres," says Huerequeque, who is not quite sober, "I know how we can do it. In Brazil I saw how a lady like this was put ashore — maybe not such a fat one, but Huerequeque has seen more of the world than all you opera singers put together. First of all, we have to brace the ship inside with beams, then the force outside must be applied at several different places at once, and then we have to send our boys into the woods again. Now we need a lot of balsa trunks. Amigos, now let Huerequeque tackle this señorita. There's nothing to be gained here by crude assaults; we need patience."

## Camisea, Edge of the Cleared Jungle

Work has stopped, almost all activity has died down. The spidery webbing of ropes still stretches up the slope, but the cables are not fully taut. Naked children are playing in the slippery clay, smoke filters out of the huts and forms a long layer among the trees, weighed down by the closeness of the air. From a distance we hear a low singing. To the left and right we can see at least two hundred huts.

A steady pounding can be heard, muffled by the dense jungle as some women work together grinding manioc in big wooden mortars. They stuff the moist, whitish pulp into a long tube woven of liana fibers, then attach it by a loop at one end to an overhanging tree branch. A stick is pulled through another loop at the bottom of the tube, and the women lean their full weight against it, tightening the mesh and forcing out the slightly poisonous liquid of the bitter manioc.

A man works his way up the slope with a huge fish on his back almost bigger than he is, heading for one of the largest huts. Staggering under the load, he climbs the stairs, consisting of a tree trunk with steps carved into it, up to the platform of the chief's hut.

## Chief's Hut

The Indian places the fish on the floor of tough bark strips. The hut is composed of a large platform with a few pots and tools, one of the typical elevated clay fireplaces, some hammocks, and the carefully braided roof above. The chief squats on the floor with some children, and beside them sit Fitzcarraldo and Jaime de Aguila. A little to the side, two women are chewing peeled pieces of the sweet manioc root. They spit the chewed stuff into a big earthenware bowl in front of them, where it has already begun to foam and ferment. The chief has invited the guests to eat, and they are having a broth of yucca and turtle. The turtle carcass lies nearby, and the children are playing with the shell and the spiked feet. There is no conversation.

Mutely the chief hands Fitzcarraldo a flat, shiny white stone that resembles a tortilla. "Salt," Jaime whispers to him. Fitzcarraldo tries to scrape some off with his machete, but the salt tortilla is hard, and nothing comes off.

"Look," says Jaime, and he takes the stone from him and stirs his soup with it like a huge spoon.

Fitzcarraldo imitates him, stirring for a long time. "Now I've made it too salty," he whispers to him after taking a taste from his bowl.

The chief pulls over a bowl of finished manioc *chicha* and hands Fitzcarraldo a pottery drinking bowl.

"You must drink it," says Jaime threateningly. "It's just fermented saliva."

Fitzcarraldo gazes for a moment at the viscous substance, which looks a little like pale, watery yoghurt, and then takes a bowlful of it. He drinks bravely, and gestures to the chief that it tastes wonderful. "My God," he says to him, smiling, "how time flies."

## Pachitea, Near the Boat

With renewed vigor, everyone is back at work. The scores of canoes have been cleared away, many dragged ashore, and big rafts made of light, pale balsa wood, lashed with lianas, float near the bow, which still leans flat against the incline of the ramp. Indians are dragging some logs of the feather-light wood under the bow, diving underwater, as others help by shoving the logs from behind. There is enormous activity. Huerequeque, who stands chest-deep in water, is in command. On deck overhead, Fitzcarraldo and his crew are fastening the heavy cables at various points farther back on deck; it is a tedious job.

We see the ship's hull at the waterline. It has, indeed, risen a bit up front; the black-marked line along the craft's belly is already slightly inclined in the water. More and more trunks are pulled below the bow, which rises slowly. Huerequeque is happy. "Even from a peasant's brain," he cries, "you'll sometimes get something clever."

"But you're no peasant," Fitzcarraldo shouts back, "you're just the finest drunkard that ever staggered over God's earth. To Huerequeque!" He grabs the basket bottle and takes a mighty swig.

## Mountain Slope, Camisea

As one man, hundreds of Jívaros start moving at the same time, and like windmills placed horizontally, the winches begin to turn. The cables tighten, one after the other, stretching and groaning.

## Pachitea, At the Boat

By means of the mass of balsa logs the ship has been raised at a sharp angle; at the stern it seems almost to drown in the water. Supporting beams have been positioned on both sides. In a neatly arranged network, the ropes lead to different spots on the side of the hull, thereby relieving the bow of the main force pulling the boat. The Amazonian figurehead now juts sharply upward.

We see the bow up close. Pulled with enormous power, the keel now presses against the ramp, which has been rubbed with lard or soft soap. The pressure increases, the whole ship sighs from deep within. Huerequeque, working like a madman, pours water on the slick trunks, and then all at once, almost with a jerk of liberation, the bow pushes up onto them.

Huerequeque yells, "It works!" Inch by inch the keel pushes up the ramp. The Indians on the slope run in circles. After ten turns, the steamboat pushes forward a hand's breadth. To the stern it is already dangling dangerously deep into the water. On the other side of the Pachitea the ropes are loosened. This is the beginning.

"We forgot something," Fitzcarraldo roars from on deck.

"What?" Huerequeque roars back.

"Enrico, Enrico Caruso," Fitzcarraldo shouts. And then a beautiful, stately aria begins and enraptures us.


## On Board, Deck, Night

Near the mess table Fitzcarraldo and his men have tied hammocks, and only Huerequeque sits at the polished mahogany table. He is already heavy and slow from a great deal of *aguardiente*. He has a glass in front of him, and he keeps putting it back in its place when it slides back toward him. With his bare chest leaned against the edge of the table, he stops the glass, refusing to acknowledge the steep slant of the table. From the way the hammocks are hanging, we can discern precisely the angle to the vertical. The men are daydreaming. Fitzcarraldo talks to his parrot Bald Eagle, but the bird just nibbles patiently at a wax candle, and doesn't say a word.

Jaime raises his voice from his hammock. "The cigarettes are going too fast, we have to ration them more carefully. And the kerosene for the lamps will be used up soon as well."

"My torchbearers will come then, my armies shall bring the light," says Wilbur, whose hammock is slung beside his abandoned barber chair. "We shall proclaim the Ucayali and the Pachitea as the Kingdom of the Jívaros, and we shall stay here forever."

"Wilbur," says Fitzcarraldo soothingly, drawing on his cigarette, which illuminates his face.

"Fitz?" says Wilbur.

"We'll stay for a very long time," says Fitzcarraldo. "How fast are we getting on?" he asks in the direction of Jaime, after a pause.

"On a good day we can manage thirty feet, like the other day, but something always interferes. Today we didn't advance at all, and yesterday it was an arm's length, if anything." A new pause ensues.

"We'll have to build ourselves a hut," says Fitzcarraldo. "This lopsided life is getting ridiculous." He looks at Huerequeque, who is trying to prop his glass with a knife handle, but the knife and the glass are now sliding toward him together. The sounds of the night drift over from the nearby forest. Otherwise it is dark all around.

## Mountain Slope, Camisea

The boat has been pulled up the slope farther than its own length. It is propped up on both sides, and additional trunks have been placed at the stern. Towed by ropes they have the effect of huge levers. Some pulleys with long chains are towing as well, and the work is in full swing. It is impressive to watch, hundreds of Indians working simultaneously at the winches, trotting in circles. The proper tempo has been found; it is no longer hectic, as it was in the very beginning. At the edge of the swath through the forest the women are working, their fireplaces burning everywhere. All told, there must be eleven hundred natives.

A large group has assembled down by the river, something is going on. We recognize Fitzcarraldo and Jaime de Aguila amongst them. Wailing sounds reach us as we overlook the scene.

About a dozen women are pounding bunches of a certain herb with clubs against peeled tree trunks, until a pasty green substance is produced. Men with spears are standing around; they have painted their faces and arms black. A woman sits on the ground, rocking the upper part of her body back and forth, singing a strange, wailing song. Something extraordinary is in preparation. Standing with his men, the chief is smeared with black as well.

From the mountain slope, where most of the Indians have ceased working, groups of men are joining them. Wilbur approaches cautiously with the boy named

McNamara. The boat, which has moved only impercep-
tibly forward, now stands completely still.

Jaime carefully takes Fitzcarraldo aside. "I'm not sure
what, but something is brewing, I don't like the looks of
this. The first time, in '96, it started the same way. Do you
know what the women are doing?"

"No," says Fitzcarraldo.

"It's a poison, a very potent one, not just for chickens,"
says Jaime.

"And the men painted in black. What does that
mean?" asks Fitzcarraldo.

"It means that they're invisible, they do that before the
hunt or going to war," Jaime explains. "But the woman
singing, I can't place that yet."

"What's she singing?" asks Fitzcarraldo. "Shouldn't
we get back to the boat and load our rifles?"

"No, you know perfectly well we wouldn't stand a
chance. Let me listen," says Jaime. "She's singing to some
kind of fertility goddess, it doesn't fit somehow. She
sings: 'Thou art a woman like me, I always call the food.
My little children, come ye to me happily, so come to me
also, my beloved food.' "

Then, all at once, life returns to the assembly. Fitzcarraldo is ready for anything, but what happens, unexpect-
edly, is this: the women spill the poison into the river, and
the men with the spears jump into canoes, and now we
realize the meaning of this mysteriousness. After a few
seconds, several big fish rise to the surface belly-up,
unconscious, twitching briefly in paralysis. The invisible

ones pierce them with their spears. In seconds, many of the nearly man-sized fish have been killed. A wave of relief now runs through Fitzcarraldo.

## Camisea, Mountain Slope

It is difficult to tell whether it is day or night, raining as it is like the Flood, in a way we have never seen before. Lightning flashes without interruption, the thunder cracks the earth in two. The water pours from the sky in an almost solid mass, nearly smothering the people and putting a heavy load on the forest. In no time the entire swath cut in the jungle has become a broad, clay-red stream, increasingly violent, a torrent rushing by. We see how the water instantly digs furrows and grooves, how it washes beneath the hull, how it carries away the supporting trunks and logs.

We recognize Fitzcarraldo and his men, like specters in this deluge, as they try to drive the Indians out into the rain. They seem reluctant, anxious, as far as we can make out through the downpour. The thunder rolls frightfully and the lightning flashes, terrifying.

In the flickering light and through the curtain of torrential rain, we can barely see a group of Jívaros who have set to work at one of the winches, but after only a few turns there is a terrible jerk, and the mooring, flooded by the red torrent, rips loose from the mud. Screams, men slip in the mud, a crash of wood drowns out the thunder, the hull breaks loose, starts to slip, wooden supports snap, mud and water splash up, the boat slides several yards down the slope. There is a horrible jolt and the sloshing water sprays everywhere. The ship stops dead and the ropes tighten and twang. Cries of pain, people hurrying, there has been an accident. In the pouring rain we see two Jívaros pinned beneath support beams ripped loose at the rear of the boat, squeezed together like victims of an earthquake. A burst of thunder hits like a grenade, then everything vanishes in the furious rain, as if it were only an evil apparition.


## Camisea, Mountain Slope, Early Morning

A misty, fresh, early morning, the birds rejoice with their infernal jubilation. On the hillside all is still, no people in sight, just smoke drifting from the huts at the edge of the swath. From there an oppressive feeling counteracts the exultation of the forest. Nearby we notice a confusion of logs, but the boat is stuck a good hundred yards up the slope from the Pachitea.

## On Board, Fitzcarraldo's Cabin

In Fitzcarraldo's cabin, his crew has gathered around him, depressed, everything but the open door looking lopsided on this inclined plane. The men are leaning in a peculiarly strained position against the cockeyed state of their world. Prolonged silence. Huerequeque tries to generate a little optimism with new suggestions.

"We will start up the engine," he says, "but instead of the propeller it will drive the anchor winch, and the ship will be wound up the mountain under its own power. And then we'll fasten a rope from the ship to the other side of the mountain, and put a huge barrel on tracks, and we could fill it little by little with water from the Ucayali. That way a counter-tension would arise, and the ship couldn't tear itself loose again. And we could even . . ."

"We have two dead men," Fitzcarraldo interrupts.

"I only meant," says Huerequeque after a pause, "that the weight from the other side could even pull our steamboat uphill."

Despite the general depression, we feel that the proposals may not be so bad, but at the moment there is no enthusiasm for them.

"Two men dead." Fitzcarraldo clings to his dark thoughts. "If that's the price, then I don't know. Something is wrong here, everything's warped."

We hear voices coming from the huts outside, the Jívaros are obviously in council; we hear the sound of a violent argument, and Jaime de Aguila tries to hear what it's about.

We see at a distance several hundred Jívaros gathered at the edge of the swath. Loud shouting, gesticulating. The gestures have lost their harmonious center.


## On Board, Center Deck, Night

Completely filled with sleeping people, the hammocks hang against the incline of the deck. Only Huerequeque snores irregularly amid the calm breathing of the sleepers. Steps come up the staircase from the lower deck, a figure bends over one of the hammocks. It is Jaime. He gently wakes up Fitzcarraldo, who needs a moment to orient himself.

"I've just been outside. Whether you believe this or not, they are all gone."

"What!" says Fitzcarraldo, waking the others, "what are you saying?"

"I had this feeling," says Jaime, "so I went out, and not a soul was there. Nothing. They're all gone."

Beside Wilbur, who has sat up in his hammock, the head of the Indian boy pops up in the hammock next to his. "Only McNamara, my footman, has remained with us," says Wilbur.

Jaime turns to the boy and speaks to him softly in Jívaro. The boy answers low and hesitantly. "He doesn't know anything," says Jaime. "I must say this can mean they are planning an attack, but it can mean a lot of other things as well. I don't really know what's going on. It's a mystery." Stunned silence spreads. There is a low wailing and croaking in the woods.


## On Board, Center Deck

A day veiled with thin clouds, a joyless rain drips thinly down. The steamboat hangs at an angle on the slope. The hammocks sway empty and dejected in a slight breeze. Some guns are lying around, always within reach. The crew lolls about idly.

Huerequeque plays his *sapo* game against himself, but he plays so badly and hits so seldom that he starts secretly cheating himself. "Two thousand eight hundred," he says, adding up the points, but everyone knows it wasn't even a thousand.

"Haven't you got anything better to do?" Fitzcarraldo yells at him out of the blue. We notice the men are getting on each other's nerves, the wait is gnawing at them. "For four days now," Fitzcarraldo says, "nothing but sapo, sapo, sapo, sapo. I can't stand it any more."

Jaime de Aguila sits on deck, carefully cleaning his toenails with a screwdriver. He says nothing. Wilbur and McNamara are the only ones who seem content, chewing on some fruit, spitting out the seeds, and lost in thought.

## Pachitea Riverbank

Fitzcarraldo, who can no longer stand being on deck, has climbed down to the riverbank. Behind him, the abandoned path of slippery clay soil stretches up through the jungle in a light rain. There the steamboat hangs on the slope; to the left and right, all life has withered away. The zebu cow has been tied near the bank and gazes with big, soft eyes at Fitzcarraldo, who scratches her on the forehead, between the horns. "We're going to have to kill you soon," he says in a low voice.

Fitzcarraldo steps onto a sandbar that has just formed; evidently the water level has dropped a little. Lost in contemplation, he gazes out across the lazy current of the river, which flows past him monotonously and incessantly. The jungle stands mute, a light rain drizzles, the melancholy river passes by. Scores of tiny spiders, colored an almost transparent brown so that they hardly stand out against the sand, arouse Fitzcarraldo's attention. They are long-legged speedsters with small bodies, and whenever Fitzcarraldo puts one foot before the other they bolt upright and run for a while. The whole sandbank is covered with them, both resting and on the run. When Fitzcarraldo stamps his foot hard with a thud in the damp sand, all the spiders, hundreds of them, like a fine, semitransparent skin over the sand, dash in a long-legged sprint down to the river. The spiders continue racing over the surface of the water, and it supports them. They race out onto the river as if they had never heard of the law of gravity.

## On Board, Center Deck, Night

All the men are standing in a line at the slanting railing. They strain their eyes and look out into the night in disbelief. We hear voices, myriad sounds, a hum of voices and noises.

We see what the men see. All along the edge of the forest, fires glow, shadows move, single shouts reverberate.

"They're back, as though nothing ever happened," says Fitzcarraldo, as if he were dreaming.

"I don't understand anything any more," says Jaime de Aguila softly. "It's all a mystery to me."

## Camisea, Mountain Slope

The work is in full swing once more, the place is teeming with people. The flat wooden beams of the winches turn steadily, the ropes creak, the boat groans gently, yet it is strangely quiet. The work proceeds in total silence. Suddenly, the smokestack of the *Molly Aida* makes a loud noise and belches a cloud of smoke, a solitary cloud that dissipates, then another one, and then dense smoke puffs out; the engine has been started, it begins rumbling and chugging steadily.

## On Deck, Bow

Fitzcarraldo and Huerequeque are standing by the anchor winch. The mechanic joins them. We see how the winch starts moving very slowly, how it begins winding up the heavy chain very slowly. The chain is stretched forward tautly, and about forty yards away the anchor is tied to a big stump with massive roots. The boat pulls itself up the mountain with the power of its own anchor winch.

"It works," says Huerequeque proudly.

"That takes the pressure off the other winches," says the mechanic.


## Camisea, Mountain Slope, As Before

A strange sight: the swath, the jungle, the smoking fires, the frenzied labor. And, in the middle of it all, on huge logs, the huge riverboat slowly rolling uphill, powered by itself under full steam. The chugging of the machinery chimes in with a grandiose music.


## Camisea, Opposite Slope Toward the Ucayali

On the opposite slope a big, makeshift metal barrel the size of a railroad car, open at the top, rests on tree trunks, which function as rollers. The impression of a railroad car is reinforced by the fact that the rollers are set on rails, which extend downhill about two full lengths of track. The container is attached by a heavy steel cable leading over a securely fastened wheel on top of the ridge to the boat on the other side.

A queue of hundreds of Jívaros is busy passing along buckets made of bark and filled with water; the line of people extends in a serpentine path down the swath to the shore of the Ucayali. The barrel is being filled little by little with water. We can see it will take days before it is full.

Fitzcarraldo and Huerequeque slip and slide as they walk along the line of Jívaros. Huerequeque is obviously proud. This is his invention, his idea. The Indians have painted broad stripes on their faces with reddish-ochre *achiote* and *uricuri*. As we pass along the queue with Fitzcarraldo, it strikes us that all of them avoid his gaze.

## Camisea, Fitzcarraldo's Hut, Evening

A new hut has been built at the edge of the swath; from the clothes, from the small wooden table with its detailed maps of the area, from the tin utensils, we know that this hut has been erected for Fitzcarraldo and his men. Otherwise, with its fireplace and hanging hammocks, it resembles the hut of the chief. Fitzcarraldo and his men crouch on the floor near the fire, having accustomed themselves to the posture of the Indians. The chief is their guest, and the boy named McNamara is with them as well. In the background, seen beyond the platform, we see the boat hanging on the slope, tied securely. It is fairly high up, and weeks must have passed. Outside, where the platform of the house almost touches the hillside, Indians are leaning on the inclined slope, silently looking inside. Wilbur lights a kerosene lamp and hangs it up as night sinks slowly down. The men eat yams, beans, and monkey meat with their fingers, like the Indians. The roasted monkeys look something like fine-limbed, naked babies, contorted into painful physical positions.

"Why are they doing this?" Fitzcarraldo keeps asking into the silence. "Why do they keep working?"

"I don't know," says Jaime, "we can only guess. I can't shake the thought that we're taking too much time for all this, four months have gone by already. Maybe we'll get the boat over the mountain, but maybe it will also be months too late and our option will have expired, and everything will have been in vain, and in the end they'll celebrate by making shrunken heads out of us."

"I don't think so," says Fitzcarraldo, "I think we're safe."

"How come?" asks Huerequeque.

"Unless I'm mistaken, I can see a sure sign," says Fitzcarraldo. "Look over there. Try to be inconspicuous, but look where I look. Do you see those hands on the railing?"

We follow their cautious glances. Meanwhile, black night has fallen outside. On the railing of the bark-covered platform we see several hands illuminated by the kerosene lamp, and the Jívaros face us from the darkness, motionless. In the black of night we can only guess where their eyes are, there is only darkness there.

Fitzcarraldo stares directly at the spot where their faces should be. At once the hands silently withdraw from the railing back into the darkness, and only a single Indian hand far to one side remains. Fitzcarraldo turns to that hand, staring into the darkness toward the obscured face. The hand remains, and Fitzcarraldo keeps staring unflinchingly. Then, after a long hesitation, a finger moves and the hand slips cautiously back into the darkness.


## Heights of Camisea

Like a familiar companion the day has also brought streaming rain, yet the mood is festive. *The ship has reached the summit.* A strange sight. Atop the highest spot on the ridge, the big steamboat sits firmly fastened, all smeared with clay, and on either side the jungle swath descends to the Pachitea and the Ucayali, its reddish clay just bottomless mud now. Hundreds of Jívaros are swarming about the hull of the boat, seized by joyous excitement like the rest. Wilbur has set his barber chair up on the crest, in the midst of the mud and rain, and presides from his throne, with his footman McNamara beside him. "I'm going to stay here," he proclaims into the tumult, "from here I shall reign over the united empire of the Jívaros."

Fitzcarraldo is sitting on the ground in the midst of the reddish mud, as a Jívaro bandages his swollen foot with a thin liana, up past the ankle. Apparently a little drunk, Fitzcarraldo sings. "Mosquitoes and fire ants and foot fungus don't matter to us," he sings, "we'll get this babe over the mountain."

Jaime de Aguila comes over and slaps his muddy hand on Fitzcarraldo's shoulder. "And even if we take two years, and it was all for nothing, we'll finish the job for its own sake."

Not far from them, where some Jívaros at the edge of the forest are breaking open a rotten tree with their axes, extracting fat white grubs and eating them at once, Huerequeque lies in the pouring rain, stupefied, dead drunk. He spreads a drenched linen sheet over himself and goes to sleep as if he were home in bed. The mechanic tries to get him to his feet, but Huerequeque just turns onto his side grumpily, wrapping himself with the sheet in the mud.

Stan has taken out a few balls and makes them dance, lost in his art, a sight we haven't seen for a long time. The rain suddenly stops and wanders off like a dark, striped wall. The sun breaks through a little, and over all the festive crowd and the strange, crazy steamboat on the mountain, a strong, gleaming rainbow appears. Overgrown with jungle, the slopes in the distance tower up into the white clouds, right into the mysterious.

## Camisea, Slope Toward the Ucayali

A normal intensive work day, but now the bow of the ship points down toward the Ucayali, and the winches are all operating behind the boat, braking it with the same power that was earlier used to pull. The Indians are all leaning against the crossbeams, now going backwards in circles. The boat has already made it a third of the way down the other side, but it seems to have reached a difficult point on the slope, where a deep furrow several yards wide must be crossed on some sort of bridge of cumbersome trunks and support beams.

Fitzcarraldo is there with his men, and bending down below the boat's belly he examines the movement of the mass. We see how the colossal hulk of the steamboat moves downward foot by foot, grating hollowly.

"I wouldn't have thought so, but downhill is just as difficult," says Fitzcarraldo.

"But now it's a little faster," says Huerequeque, "so we must have learned something."

## Banks of the Ucayali

Again there is rain, but what a moment. The boat lies tied to a ramp, with its bow almost touching the light, clay-colored waters of the Ucayali. The river is carrying high water and streaming by at a terrible speed; leaves and wood float on the surface, the sign of a rapidly rising flood.

Eleven hundred Jívaros drag their canoes in a strange procession down the mountainside to the Ucayali, where the terrain is somewhat flatter than on the Pachitea side.

Fitzcarraldo stands, axe in hand, by a tightly stretched rope, and gives his men a sign, to Wilbur, to Stan, to Jaime, to the others. Axes, machetes swoop down as they start hacking in turns, and with a final mighty chop, Fitzcarraldo cuts the last rope, stretched so tightly it bursts. With a clumsy, hollow wobble, the boat begins to move, sluggishly picks up speed, and finally slides with the full force of its weight into the Ucayali. The bow dives deep into the water and, a moment later, the boat rights itself on the brownish, foaming flood. This is its true launching, and amid the rejoicing Huerequeque gleefully fires his rifle, though its sound is drowned out by shouting and singing. The boat, with ropes still fixed to the bow, now turns parallel to the shore, where Fitzcarraldo's men tie it up at once in front and back. The bow faces against the current.

As proud as a father after the birth of his first son, Fitzcarraldo lights himself a cigar, his last one, he says, and at once serves *aguardiente* in great quantity, taking a whole bowlful for himself. We've never seen him like this, so beside himself, so totally given over to the joy of the moment. And how this man can be happy is a pleasure to watch.

"Three weeks early," cries Huerequeque in front of him, "three weeks before the deadline!"

"Yes," says Fitzcarraldo, "we've done it. Watch out, now comes the official part."

He makes a meaningful pause. "We need a harbor." Then he roars with laughter, "I'll found a town here! A hammer, quick! And stakes, and ropes!"

Someone hands Fitzcarraldo the things he needs. He races madly back and forth on the shore, hammering on poles, tying ropes and uttering wild, snorting sounds of joy. "This here will be the marketplace," he cries, "and that will be the mayor's office, and Main Street will run in this direction, and here I'll build my palace, and here we'll have a small theater, and here . . ."

"What'll you call this town?" asks Wilbur, awestruck.

Fitzcarraldo stops short in his creative raving. His face is marked with enthusiasm, bright with happiness. He makes a very sly face. "*Fitzcarraldo*," says Fitzcarraldo.

Indescribable cheering breaks loose and, as if they understood, the Jívaros cautiously join in. Wilbur is overcome by one of his seductive ecstasies. "I'll weave you a hammock of living snakes!" he sings.

## Banks of the Ucayali, Toward Evening

Pressing close to one another, Fitzcarraldo, his men, and the eleven hundred Jívaros are gathered on the bank of the Ucayali, which in the meantime has risen another three feet or more. The boat, however, lies securely tied at the riverbank. Fitzcarraldo is already rather drunk, he staggers with wobbly knees over to the chief and tries to shake his hand, but the chief simply touches his hand softly with his fingertips. The Indians are strangely silent now, they seem introverted, their gaze turns within. Over everything, Caruso's voice resounds. Dusk sinks down on this scene.


## Fitzcarraldo's Cabin, Early Morning

Fitzcarraldo lies in bed, sleeping off his drunk. From outside we listen to the voices of the jungle as they announce a fresh morning. The water of the river rushes and slaps the side of the ship. But the water is curiously loud, and the voices of the birds sound strangely hollow, like an echo. The boat shakes slightly, then it begins to sway. Fitzcarraldo's bed sways so much that his body rolls slowly back and forth. His bed keeps rocking up and down as if it were bobbing on the high seas amid heavy swells.

Fitzcarraldo wakes up all green in the face, hung over. He feels his head, his forehead is buzzing, the cabin is turning in circles, the floor is uncertain as it rocks up and down, his bed slides to and fro. He gets ready to vomit but, suddenly waking to full awareness, he realizes it is not his head vibrating and going in circles, it is the cabin that is rocking. *The whole boat is rocking.* Fitzcarraldo flies out of bed.

He dashes on deck, dressed only in his trousers. A few Jívaros are huddling on board, but that is not it: *The boat is drifting pilotless* down the Ucayali, and a moment later he realizes it's much worse than that, much more terrifying, there can be no doubt: the boat is drifting right into the Pongo das Mortes. For a second or two, Fitzcarraldo stares in disbelief — distraught. The dramatic cliffs jut up to the left and right, and up ahead they narrow to the gorge through the rocks.

At the same moment, Jaime de Aguila comes racing on deck as well.

"The Pongo!" cries Fitzcarraldo with a voice no longer human, "we're drifting into the Pongo!" The Indians sit motionless, staring into their profoundest depths, their eyes as wide and empty as the sea. The boat is reeling.


## Engine Room

Fitzcarraldo and Jaime hurry down to the engine room in a panic. They must grope for support with their hands as they are thrown from side to side with the lurching of the boat. The floor is slippery with oil.

Jaime falls and staggers up again. "The valves first! Open the valves!" he shouts.

"Where?" cries Fitzcarraldo desperately.

At that moment the mechanic comes slipping down the narrow iron staircase. "Open the boiler, start the fire, quick!" he commands.

## Pongo das Mortes, Early Morning

It is high water in the Pongo, and it is even more terrifying than we remember. It roars and rages and thunders, and already the ship comes drifting at a frightful speed, hurled forward by the waves, whirled in circles by the swirling current, pilotless, ripped along by the elements. Foaming white waves loom up in rage, the boat rises on the towering waves and comes shooting down again into a bottomless valley.

And then, all at once, smoke starts coming from the smokestack, cautiously at first, then thicker and fuller, and the smokestack, tossed to and fro, draws weird patterns of smoke in the gorge. But it is too late, no power in the world could now stop the *Molly Aida*'s voyage to hell. Then, in a narrow bend, there is a vile, atrocious, sick scraping sound as the ship smashes against a rocky wall, part of the superstructure rips away at once, then there is a crash, a muffled rumbling, and the elements hurl the ship through the foaming white maelstrom.


## Pongo das Mortes, Lower End

The Pongo das Mortes lies there before us, raging, the rocky walls above veiled in mists. And then, all of a sudden, it spits out the *Molly Aida*, which now lists in the water lopsided, smoking heavily. Its upper housing is torn apart in front, but somehow it is still afloat. How it was possible to come out of this unharmed strikes us as a miracle. Behind the boat the Pongo roars like a hundred thousand stags in heat, so proud of its monstrous power.

And as the boat drifts towards us, having survived the inferno, we have time to let a terrible thought germinate. Here comes Fitzcarraldo, emerging from the lower end of the Pongo, and so everything was to no avail. Yes, *everything was to no avail*. And: *why, then,* how could this happen, why was the boat set adrift? The dream is over, all was in vain. In a single night, eight months of exertion are rendered null and void. Fitzcarraldo again ends up below the Pongo das Mortes.


## On Board, Below the Pongo das Mortes

Parts of the upper deck are dangling down onto the center decks, and it looks like the aftermath of battle. Fitzcarraldo is dazed, he hasn't fully grasped what has happened. This stroke of misfortune was too severe. Jaime, bleeding at the mouth after hurting himself somehow, questions the Indians on board, just four of them, who report to him with happy, relaxed faces. Yes, they seem relieved, almost overjoyed.

"Now just sit down and hold on," says Jaime. "Do you know what they are saying? Fitz, grab hold of something. They say they untied the boat themselves last night, so we would drift downstream all night long, and they did it on purpose. They say they always knew our boat, the divine vessel, was only dragged over the mountain so it could drift through the rapids. They say it was necessary, that they had been waiting for this since the time of their forefathers, it was necessary to reconcile the evil spirits of the rapids." The Indians nod in affirmation. They are quite relieved and happy, and start singing a song.

The boat limps toward the shore where, in the distance, we recognize Don Aquilino's settlement.


## Don Aquilino's Settlement

Fitzcarraldo and Don Aquilino are sitting on the veranda of the house. Fitzcarraldo is silent, almost catatonic. Don Aquilino makes an effort to help his guest get over the worst. But he is discreet in doing this and, to a certain degree, sensitive. He opens a bottle of champagne.

"First of all, have a drink. Taming the Pongo das Mortes with a steamboat is a record that won't be repeated."

He turns to the Indians and hands them a glass of champagne. "Formidable gentlemen," he cries, "to the soothing of the evil spirits of the Pongo."

Fitzcarraldo remains silent.

"Look here," continues Don Aquilino, "out in front of the house, all the way down to the Ucayali, those are all champagne bottles, there's always a reason to celebrate here."

We see that the road leading down to the river really is paved with champagne bottles, that is, empty bottles have been stuck in the ground in such a way that the bottoms form a paved road. At the Ucayali, Fitzcarraldo's boat is moored; in the distance we can see his crew removing the upper structures.

"To the Pongo das Mortes," says Don Aquilino, raising his glass. Fitzcarraldo raises his without a word and drinks it down.

"What will you do now?" asks Don Aquilino.

Silence. Fitzcarraldo shrugs his shoulders.

"You know," says Don Aquilino, "I ask you that because I am interested in your boat, since for you it's of no use any more, while I myself could put it to good use. The business here has expanded a great deal lately. The hull and the engine have weathered the Pongo quite well, and within a week it should be possible to mend the damage. I assure you I don't mean to exploit your delicate situation. . . ."

But Fitzcarraldo doesn't react properly, he is far away in his thoughts, where there is nothing but darkness.

Don Aquilino feels rather helpless with his guest and his misfortune. He tries to direct the conversation to more pleasant topics.

"From Manaus we have news of a European opera company that is giving a guest performance there at the moment, perhaps you should go there, I mean to relax. They say that there's an opera by a sensational German composer there, one of the very modern ones, Federico . . . no, Ricardo, what's his name? Ricardo Wagner, I think, and the opera is called *Walkiria,* one of those fat Teutonic goddesses, the whole thing is supposed to be very Teutonic."

Suddenly life returns to Fitzcarraldo, first to his eyes, then he sits erect. "Wagner," he says, "really? The one who wrote *Parsifal?*"

"It must be the same one," says Don Aquilino.

"Tell me," says Fitzcarraldo, "about the boat, do you really mean it?" A sudden idea has seized him, he has caught fire. The fire has taken possession of Fitzcarraldo again.


## Ucayali, Near Don Aquilino's Settlement

Don Aquilino and Fitzcarraldo are coming down the road paved with French champagne bottles, toward the landing where the *Molly Aida* is moored. Fitzcarraldo is cheerful and full of energy, clutching a bundle of money in his hands. Upon arriving at the boat he calls his crew together. Now we see the devastation on the upper deck more closely; no vital elements seem to have been affected, although the boat is looking rather desolate.

"My friends," says Fitzcarraldo to his men who, surprised by his effusive mood, have flocked around him, "may I present to you the new owner of the *Molly Aida,* Don Aquilino. But he has agreed to a clause that permits us to keep the boat for our own use for two more weeks. We'll patch it up temporarily. Jaime, you will travel to Manaus, you'll take a boat and all the money here, you'll bring me back a tailcoat, and the biggest cigar in the world, and from the theater an armchair with velvet upholstery. I've made a promise to a pig that loves Caruso so much."

"Yes," says Jaime.

Fitzcarraldo makes a very secretive face and whispers in his ear: "*And then. . . .*"

## Ucayali, Landing

It is early morning, one of the most spectacular, blazing up beyond the jungle in red flames. Quiet flows the river. We look downstream. All at once several *peke-pekes* appear from the next bend of the Ucayali, a small flotilla of seven or eight boats, chugging up the river in a broad formation.

Fitzcarraldo is standing at the gangplank of the *Molly Aida,* which has been roughly put in order; at least a week must have passed. Fitzcarraldo is looking hard, he recognizes Jaime in the lead boat, waving, and Fitzcarraldo draws a deep breath: Here they come.

The boats land, and now they come thronging ashore, exhausted, yes, but also exhilarated by the unusual boat trip: the musicians, the singers, *the entire orchestra.*

"We shall make our entry into Iquitos, we shall bring Grand Opera to Iquitos," Fitzcarraldo calls out, "*just once in my life.*" And then the sounds of the jungle vanish, the noises of the boats, the speech of man. Grandly the overture of the *Walküre* sets in, the music pervades everything, the landscape, the heart.

We see Fitzcarraldo greeting the conductor with a handshake, helping the singers, mighty Germanic women, on land, as Jaime de Aguila hands over a cigar of unheard-of proportions, a theater seat, and a tailcoat. And then the sound swells up, the music grows, becoming all-embracing. A small pudgy Italian bassist is suddenly bereft of his instrument, which is drifting away — an accident while unloading. With its wide belly, the double bass floats away on the Ucayali. The little Italian is sobbing after it, inconsolably.


## Mouth of the Ucayali, at the Amazon

There goes the *Molly Aida,* steaming proudly past us down the Ucayali into the mighty Amazon. There it turns upstream in a wide curve, in the direction of Iquitos. All of this has something uplifting about it, a pathos, a grandeur. The music increases, the singing begins, and we see that the entire upper platform is occupied by the orchestra, there the male and female singers stand with helmet, spear, and armor, imposing Germanic deities, singing.

They have erected a forest of papier maché, their theater sets and the stage forest pass by the real jungle. What a sight!

## On Board

There lies Fitzcarraldo, slouched in his hammock, in tailcoat and laced shirt, smoking *the biggest cigar in the world*, and beside him he has the empty velvet chair from the Teatro Amazonas in Manaus. Next to him lies Wilbur in his barber's throne with his eyes closed. And the orchestra plays the *Walküre*.

## Iquitos

The riverbank of Iquitos resembles an excited beehive, people are streaming together in countless numbers, like a brushfire a shout spreads through town: Fitzcarraldo's coming back. But a miracle seems to have happened; Fitzcarraldo, who had been lost for eight months, who disappeared upstream, is coming back from downstream! How is that possible? It can't be, someone who's gone upstream *has to come back from upstream*! A miracle, something incomprehensible has happened. Thousands of excited people rush together. The shore is black with people.

We recognize Molly running up with some of her girls, and how happy she is! Fitzcarraldo has returned. And Bronski is standing there, pale and quiet, staring straight ahead downstream. Music is wafting over from the river, the *Walküre*.

## Amazon River

We see the *Molly Aida* still at a distance, proudly steaming along, the boat following its course upriver in its last triumph.

## On Board

The music plays, swelling again into a great, painful jubilation. We see Fitzcarraldo stretched out in his tailcoat with the biggest cigar in the world. He makes his entry into Iquitos like a real king, just once in his life he has brought Grand Opera to this city.

Then, suddenly, a voice above him squawks over the music. "Birds are smart," says the voice, "but they cannot speak." Fitzcarraldo spins around. And there his parrot perches above him on the railing of the upper deck, almost featherless, with the bald ass; we had almost forgotten him, not having seen him for such a long time. He looks down at Fitzcarraldo, his head to one side.

"You little bastard," says Fitzcarraldo, "there you are again. I think I'll have to teach you a new sentence: 'There is no sin beyond the equator,' " he says to the bird.

The shore comes into view, people are running along with the boat, trying to keep up. The boats appear, the huts, the town. The music of the *Walküre* drowns out everything else. Fitzcarraldo is puffing up a cloud. He makes his entry into Iquitos, a king makes his entry, and he brings Grand Opera with him.

*And Fitzcarraldo rejoices.*

This book was set in Mergenthaler Cloister, a typeface designed by Morris Benton in the early twentieth century, based on the "perfect roman letter" of the fifteenth-century French mintmaster Nicolas Jenson, who flourished in Venice around 1470. Cloister is included in the Venetian family of typefaces.

Typography by Accent & Alphabet, Berkeley, California
Printed on acid-free paper by Spilman Printing, Sacramento, California